SNAG

I'M DREAMING OF
A RIGHT CHRISTMAS

SNAG

I'M DREAMING OF A RIGHT CHRISTMAS

DAVE AND NETA JACKSON

STORY AND CHARACTERS BASED ON THE MINI-MOVIE™ OF THE SAME NAME. STORY BY GEORGE TAWEEL & ROB LOOS, TELEPLAY BY MARTHA WILLIAMSON

BROADMAN
& HOLMAN
PUBLISHERS

Nashville, Tennessee

Copyright © 1994

BROADMAN & HOLMAN PUBLISHERS

TAWEEL-LOOS & COMPANY ENTERTAINMENT
"The mini-movie™ Studio"

"SNAG" is based on the characters created by
George Taweel & Rob Loos. Story by George Taweel & Rob Loos.
Teleplay written by Meredith Siler. © 1994.
Text illustrations by Anderson Thomas Design, Inc., and
Julian Jackson

4240-07
0-8054-4007-0

Dewey Decimal Classification: JF
Subject Heading: Human Relations—Fiction
Library of Congress Card Catalog Number: 94-38431
Printed in the United States of America

Library of Congress Cataloging-in-Publication Data
Jackson, Dave. 1944—
    SNAG : "I'm dreaming of a right Christmas" / by Dave and
Neta Jackson.
        p. cm. — (Secret adventures ; #5)
    "Based on the video of the same name created by George
Taweel & rob Loos."
    Summary: While enduring the dirty tricks of her enemy Arlene
during the Christmas season, Drea discovers the true meaning of
the season.
    ISBN 0-8054-4007-0 : $4.99
    [1. Christmas—Fiction.]   I. Jackson, Neta.   II. Title.   III.
Series: Jackson, Dave, 1944—   Secret adventures ; #5.
PZ7.J132418Shg   1994
[Fic]—dc20   94-38431
                                                         CIP
                                                          AC

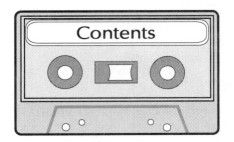

Contents

Let us not love with words or tongue but with actions and in truth.

—1 John 3:18, NIV

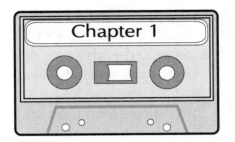

I'm Dreaming of a White Christmas

Deck the halls! Notify St. Nick! School's out! All riiiight!

Hi, E.D. Since I'm using my Walkman as an *electronic diary*—otherwise known as "E.D."—I should note that today is Day 4,937 in the Secret Adventures of yours truly, Drea Thomas . . . and man, I thought Winter Break would never get here. Nobody warned me that the first semester of seventh grade would seem like two years on a roller coaster.

But finally . . . a two-week vacation! Umm . . . just one little *SNAG*. The calendar and the weatherman seem to have gotten their wires crossed. Christmas is only a week away . . . but it's a little hard to get in the holiday spirit when the weather is a balmy sixty-two degrees! In fact, it was so warm a couple of the eighth-grade girls wore short-shorts and flip-flops decorated with jingle bells to school . . . creating a minor riot in the hallway until Mrs. Long, the principal, sent them home to change.

Grandpa said he heard on the radio that this is the warmest December in Hampton Falls since 1906. Huh! Who cares about setting records for the most tropical Christmas north of the Mason-Dixon line? Not me. I was born and raised in Hampton Falls, New Jersey, and it just doesn't seem like Christmas without snow!

Oh, well. Snow or no snow, I've still got to baby-sit the principal's kids today as usual . . . which is NOW, if the pitter-patter of little feet coming up the stairs is any clue—no, make that a thundering herd of buffaloes!

Over and out, E.D.

— Click! —

Dear E.D. . . . It's Saturday, Day 4,938 in the Secret Adventures of Drea Thomas . . . Temperature: fifty-five and climbing . . . Time: Oh-nine-hundred hours . . . (That's nine o'clock in the morning to common civilians.) Place: the kitchen . . . and I'm getting a quick breakfast while waiting for Mrs. Long to pick me up and drop me off with Matt and Rebecca at the mall. In a moment of holiday insanity last night I offered to take them shopping today . . . ya know, so they could buy gifts for their mom without her being along. Oh, well. I need to get started on my own gift list, anyway.

Just hope I get back in time to get our tree today. Grandpa always comes over to help decorate— that's been a tradition ever since he retired from the railroad several years ago, and I can't wait!

Speaking of a list, where did I put . . . ? Oh, here it is. Let's see . . . I need gifts for Dad and Mom, of course, and Grandpa, and Matt and Rebecca, and Kimberly—she's my best friend, after all—and . . . I wonder if I should get George Easton something? He's a pretty good friend, too . . . nah, guess not. Wish this friendship business with a guy wasn't so weird sometimes . . .

Wait a minute . . . what's that burning smell . . . ? Aiiiee! My toast!

Whirling toward the kitchen counter, I dive for the plug of our 1952 Sunbeam toaster, the Baron of Burned Bagels.

"You burned my breakfast!" I say accusingly, digging the charred remains of a bagel out of Mr. Toaster's slots.

"Humph. Just trying to get your attention, Drea," Mr. Toaster pouts. "I didn't hear MY name on your Christmas list . . . even toasters have feelings, you know."

Oh, brother. That's what I get for having imaginary conversations with talking toasters.

"Okay, Toaster," I sigh, trying to scrape my "Burnt Black" bagel to a "Toasted Tan." "What do you want for Christmas?"

"Well, I was thinking a bow tie and dinner

jacket might be nice . . . ya know, to go out on the town now and then." Mr. Toaster grins and does a little two-step on the counter.

"A new toaster timing device from the hardware store sounds like a better idea to me," I interrupt, holding up my "well-done" bagel in Mr. Toaster's face. "I'm tired of scraping burnt bagels when I ordered them lightly browned!"

Just then a familiar voice invades my verbal duel with the toaster. "Somebody need a ride to the hardware store?"

Oh . . . hi, Mom! . . . No, I don't need to go to the hardware store . . . just talking to myself. Hey— what are you doing all dressed for work? It's Saturday!

— Click! —

Back again, E.D. Boy, what a bummer. Mom has to work at Jamison's Department Store today—it's the Only-Eight-More-Shopping-Days-Till-Christmas-Frenzy for Mom and her marketing department. Not only that, she said Dad has already gone to work at the college—they've still got four more days of school next week that he's gotta prepare for.

Sigh. Another *SNAG.* So much for getting our tree and decorating it today—

Honnnnnk.

Oops, there's a horn in the driveway. Gotta jet . . . wish me luck on our shopping expedition! Over and out, E.D.

— Click! —

Still Day 4,938 . . . According to my neon-colored watch—which, with a *little* imagination likes to morph military time—it's now fifteen-thirty hours—that's 3:30 P.M. to monotonous mortals . . . and I'm flat on my back on my bed under the attic eaves, barely able to move. *Groan* . . . my Christmas vacation is only one day old and already I look like the poster girl for those "Shop Till You Drop" commercials.

I couldn't believe the crowds at the mall, E.D.! Everybody and their Great-Aunt Bessie must have waited until this weekend to do Christmas shopping. 'Course, I should talk . . . I haven't bought a thing yet . . . and already my feet are killing me!

Wait . . . I think we have Grandpa Ben's electric foot massager around here someplace. We gave it to him for Christmas last year to use when his feet hurt after working in the garden—ya see, E.D., he doesn't have a garden 'cause he lives in an apartment, so he's adopted ours. But he says the massager shakes so much his teeth rattle. Still, I think I'll give it a try. Be back in a sec, E.D. . . . uhhhh, *if* I can get off this bed.

— Click! —

Back again, E.D. Ahhhhhhhhhh . . . that really feels good. While my feet get an electric massage, I can catch you up on what went down when I took Matt and Rebecca Christmas shopping today . . . or should I say, "supposedly" took them shopping.

The kids were really cranked up, and I have to admit their excitement was contagious. At first it was fun walking around the mall. All the store windows were decorated with evergreen boughs, big red ribbons, and twinkling lights, and Salvation Army volunteers were ringing their bells at every corner . . . it definitely set a holiday mood—even if all the shoppers *were* in short sleeves. But I didn't really have time to look at the decorations, because Matt and Rebecca dragged me to every toy store in sight.

Just when I thought we'd seen every action figure, video game, and electronic gizmo in the state of New Jersey, Matt spied a display for the Mighty Morphin Power Rangers.

"Oh, Drea!" he said, pulling me toward the brightly-lit display. "Do you think Mom would get me a Mega-Zord for Christmas? "Power Rangers" is my favorite TV show!" And he demonstrated his best karate side kick, right there in the store aisle.

Now, just in case some great-grandchild of mine is listening to this tape in A.D. 2074 and wonders if I'm talking gibberish, I gotta explain Power Rangers. It's a TV show that's really popular right now, about some hip teenagers who've been given superpowers to karate chop the bad guys. Matt loves it—especially since he started taking karate lessons. My dad says he hopes it will soon fade away along with Cabbage Patch Dolls and the hula hoop . . . not a bad idea.

Anyway. As for this Mega-Zord that Matt wants, it's a dinosaur robot "thing" that's kinda hard to describe. It looks sorta like a triceratops . . . no, more like a saber-toothed tiger . . . hmmm, maybe a pterodactyl.

Rebecca saw me eyeballing the weird monster and sighed. "A Mega-Zord," she explained patiently, "is all the Dino Zord robots that the Power Rangers ride snapped together to create one—you know—*mega* Zord."

"Yeah!" said Matt.

"Oh," I grinned. As I stared at the mega-whatzit and the blue, yellow, red, pink, and black action figures in the display, my imagination kinda flipped the ON switch . . .

"So!" said the Red Power Ranger, sleek and muscular in his red body suit, standing with hands on hips and feet apart. "You think you're good enough to be a Power Ranger, do you?"

"Who . . . me?" I said, astonished.

All the other action figures suddenly cracked up, rolling around the toy display, laughing and holding their sides.

"Very amusing," said the Red Power Ranger, keeping his composure. "I mean the kid there . . . Matt Long."

Matt's eyes widened. "Me? A Power Ranger?" And suddenly Matt the Mighty Seven-Year-Old had morphed into Matt the Power Ranger, complete with a purple body suit and a dino "helmet" that looked suspiciously like a cross between the duck-billed snout of a hadrosaurus and Matt's blue and red baseball cap.

"All riiiiight!" Matt said and did two quick karate chops in the air.

"Not so fast," said the Red Ranger. The other Rangers lined up on either side of their leader, hands on hips, feet apart. "You have to meet the Power Ranger code . . ."

"What's that?" said Matt, practically slobbering in his eagerness. "I'll do anything!"

"Anything?" said the Red Ranger slyly. "Good . . . first, ask your mom to buy all the Power Ranger action figures for Christmas, PLUS the Mega-Zord, then . . ."

"O—kay, I think we've seen enough," I said hastily, prying Matt away from the toy display. Honestly, E.D., sometimes my imagination seems to have a life of its own!

"Hey, Matt, didn't you say you'd already asked your mom for commando robots, a launching pad, *and* a space module?" I reminded him. "I mean . . . do you realize how much all of that is going to cost?"

Matt shrugged. "But it's Christmas! Kids are supposed to get lots of presents under the tree."

"Drea's right," Rebecca jumped in, glaring at her little brother through her wire rim glasses. "You're being greedy, Matt. Besides, if you get all those things, then how is Mom going to afford to get me a CD player?"

We seemed to be hitting a definite *SNAG* in the concept of Christmas shopping. "Say, guys," I said, "didn't you come down here to buy some Christmas gifts? I mean, don't you want to look for something for your mom? And what about your grandma . . . and your teacher at school?"

Matt stuffed his hands in his jean pockets and stared at his toes. "I know," he said, "but it's just that I keep seeing stuff I want for myself."

"Yeah," Rebecca admitted.

"Well, come on, let's look at some stores your mom might be interested in," I suggested, pulling them toward Timbuktu Limited, which had some great-looking imported scarves in the window. Matt wanted to buy one with purple pigs on it, but Rebecca said, "No way!" She held up some dangly silver earrings, but Matt said they looked like flattened tin cans.

Next we tried Kitchen Korner ("Boring," said Matt) and Blue Moon Book Shop ("That's school stuff," complained Rebecca) . . . so finally I gave up. It was already way past lunch time, so we bought three big slices of pizza at Food Circus—ya know, that section of the mall populated with half a trillion fast-food counters—and had just finished mopping pizza sauce off our chins when we ran into Arlene Blake and Marcy Mannington . . . literally.

Frankly, E.D., it's bad enough having to put up

with Arlene's putdowns at school without ruining my Christmas vacation, too. But we couldn't exactly avoid it . . . Marcy—Arlene's ever-present "shadow"—was loaded down with about six shopping bags and ran right into me as they were coming out of Flashions.

"Watch where you're going, Thomas!" Arlene snapped. As usual, our infamous class president looked like a magazine cover from *Seventeen* in her red stirrup pants, white turtleneck, and red-and-white knit top. It's amazing, E.D., how she manages to keep up her image as the most popular girl in seventh grade . . . even on a *Saturday*, during *vacation*.

I tried to ignore Arlene and turned to Marcy, who was shuffling the heavy shopping bags. "Sorry, Marcy . . . looks like you've got a lot of your Christmas shopping done already."

Marcy shrugged. "Not really," she said. "These are Arlene's gifts . . . *for* Arlene from her folks, I mean."

Matt immediately looked interested. "Really?" he said. "Do your parents always let you buy your own Christmas gifts, Arlene?"

"Of course," Arlene said, tossing her head in that irritating, superior way she has. "It saves me the hassle of returning everything."

I was dumbfounded. "But . . . doesn't it take all of the surprise out of Christmas morning?" I asked.

"Don't be silly," Arlene sniffed. "My folks are always surprised when they see what they got me." She checked a list she held in her hand. "Come on, Marcy . . . I'm only half done. We can't waste anymore time dawdling with losers"—Arlene looked at our empty hands—"who can't seem to make smart decisions, even at Christmas."

Honestly! I thought, watching them go. What was Christmas coming to when people like Arlene buy their own Christmas presents? But she *was* right about one thing: we weren't having much luck shopping, so finally we caught the next bus home.

"Well," I said, trying to be optimistic as I dropped Matt and Rebecca off at their house empty-handed, "at least you got some gift ideas to think about, okay?"

But frankly, E.D., shopping with those two was exhausting. All I heard was "I want this" and "I want that," until I thought I was going to—

Riiiiiiinnnnnnnnnng.

Uh . . . the phone . . .

North Pole, Rudolph speaking . . . oh, hi, Grandpa!

— *Click!* —

That was Grandpa Ben, E.D. He offered to drive me to the Christmas tree lot and help me pick out a nice tree since both Mom and Dad are working today. I'm kinda disappointed that we're not all going together—I mean, we *always* go pick out our Christmas tree together, but . . . I guess this'll be okay. We can set it up tonight, and then all of us can decorate it after church tomorrow.

Good ol' Grandpa . . . always manages to save the day in one way or another. Now, if I could only plug this electric foot massager into his car somehow . . .

Over and out.

— Click! —

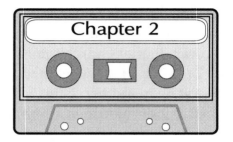

Chapter 2

Deck the Halls

It's now Sunday night, E.D., and the house looks so Christmasy! The inside, that is . . . Dad and Grandpa are outside having a race to see who can be first putting up the lights on the outside of the house.

Anyway. While they're finishing the decorating, I'll tell you about the absolutely primo tree Grandpa and I picked out yesterday! It's about eight feet tall and fits perfectly in the living room by the arch into the music room. That way it can be seen from both rooms. Mom and Dad were so surprised to see it all set up, ready to decorate, when they got home from work last night.

After church today, we finally got down to serious decorating. It was so much fun digging familiar decorations out of the Christmas boxes . . . like those lumpy dough ornaments I made in kindergarten that Mom insists on putting on the tree *every* year. Mom and I draped the artificial evergreen garlands over the living room mirror and up the stairway bannister, while Dad strung lights on the tree and Grandpa set up the manger scene on the fireplace mantle.

Mom's really into red bows again this year, so besides the lights and ornaments on the tree, she tied red velvet bows on all the branches. Have to admit, it looks kinda cool.

Each year we save putting the angel on the top of the tree till the very last. Since we all wanted to do it, we had to draw straws . . . Grandpa won. The angel has a light inside that plugs into the tree lights, and when Dad flipped the switch, the sequins and glitter on the angel's robe and wings sparkled on the ceiling.

Then we *always* make a fire in the fireplace after our yearly Decorating Marathon . . . and even though the temperature is hovering near sixty again, Dad insisted on making his "hot chocolate special." While Mom was helping him in the kitchen, Grandpa and I brought in wood from the garage for the fire.

"It's not very cold, Grandpa," I said, dumping my logs into the wood bin. "Do you think we should still build a fire?"

"Sure," Grandpa said, chuckling. "We can always open the windows or turn on the air conditioning."

"Yeah, right," I said, making a face at him. I watched while Grandpa laid the kindling and stacked the logs neatly on the grate.

"Ah, can't wait to put a match to this fire," he said. "I've been waiting for months to bid the old cherry tree a fond farewell."

Suddenly I wasn't so sure I wanted a fire after all. "Yeah, but . . . I felt sad when we cut it down last summer," I said. "I sure loved that cherry tree . . . remember when you built me a clubhouse in it?"

"Sure I do." Grandpa nodded wryly. "Especially when you fell out and your Mom and Dad nearly disowned me."

"Hey!" I protested. "I did *not* fall . . . I *jumped*. I'll have you know that was a very important day in my youthful development."

Grandpa stacked another log on the grate and rocked back on his heels. "This I gotta hear," he chuckled.

Suddenly a breeze seemed to pick me up and whirl me back . . . back . . . back to the fall when I was eight years old, playing in the old cherry tree in the back yard. Except it wasn't a cherry tree to me . . . it had transformed into a single engine airplane,

and I was Amelia Earhart flying solo across the ocean.

My plane and I flew through blinding thunder-storms, dodged hailstones big as baseballs, watched the sun come up after a long, sleepless night . . . . Nothing stopped Amelia.

And then . . . the airplane engine sputtered and died.

"Mayday! Mayday!" I cried into my two-way radio.

Silence. The radio was dead.

Hey, no problem, I thought. I just put on my trusty parachute, opened the door of the crippled plane, and stepped out over the wide expanse of blue sea . . .

. . . "Yep," I said to Grandpa. "That was the day I learned the difference between imagination and reality . . . between having a fantastic, vibrant, wildly creative, make-believe adventure . . . and actually diving head first from a cherry tree into a little pile of leaves."

Grandpa was stuffing wood chips and splinters under the pile of logs for tinder. "Yeah . . . and that lesson cost ya fourteen stitches and a broken arm," he said. Then his voice got all husky. "I'll never forget carrying you to the car in my arms and laying you in the back seat."

I remembered Grandpa's strong arms lifting me up and holding me close, even though my arm hurt like crazy and blood was all over my face. "Yeah," I said dreamily. "That was great."

Grandpa glared at me. "What?! . . . that was scary."

"Well, yeah, but . . . don't you remember?" I said. "You called your boss at the railroad and told him you couldn't leave me. They held up an entire train until my arm was in a cast! I . . . I felt so important . . . so loved."

Grandpa struck a match and held it to the tinder. Tiny flames flickered . . . caught . . . and soon were licking at the bigger kindling and logs. As he stared at the fire, I heard Grandpa mutter something to himself, something like, " 'Let us not love with words or tongue but with actions and in truth.' "

"What did you say, Grandpa?" I asked. It sounded like one of Great-Grandpa Thomas's favorite Bible verses that Grandpa is always quoting.

But Grandpa just looked at me with a funny look on his face. "I love you, Drea," he said . . . and he held out his arms wide.

"I love you, too, Grandpa," I said, scrambling into his arms and giving him a big hug back.

At that point Mom and Dad came into the living room with a tray of Dad's Double Rich Hot Chocolate and some store-bought Christmas cookies, and we all sat around the fireplace, laughing and sweating and eating. Dad was starting in on his thirteenth cookie when Grandpa clapped him on the shoulder and said, "Well, Son, how about a little race? Bet I can get the Christmas lights up around the balcony railing before you can get them up around the porch."

That got Dad out of his chair. "You're on, Dad," he said, rubbing his hands gleefully. "But no fair starting till I get the ladder up."

Say ... speaking of putting up the outside lights, Dad and Grandpa have been out there an awful long time. I wonder who's winning—

Help! What was that yell? Sounded like something from a bad Tarzan movie!

— *Click!* —

Oh, no, E.D.! Dad saw that Grandpa was almost done with the balcony, so he stretched to attach the last couple of lights without moving the ladder . . . and he and the ladder ended up in the bushes. Mom is trying to pack his sprained ankle in ice, but Dad's begging for the heating pad. Hmm. Wonder if this foot massager would help?

— *Click!* —

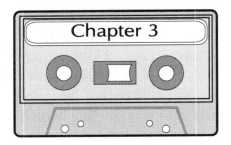

Nutcracker "Sweet"

Checkin' in, E.D. . . . Monday morning, Day 4,940 in the Secret Adventures of Drea Thomas . . . and Dad's ankle is much better today. You could hardly tell that he was limping when he went to work this morning. Frankly, E.D., I think his ego is more bruised than his ankle.

Anyway . . . Mrs. Long called a few minutes ago and wanted to know if I could baby-sit Matt and Rebecca this afternoon as usual, even though school is out. I said okay because she *promised* I wouldn't have to take them Christmas shopping. Besides, I could use a little more money for all the Christmas gifts I still need to buy.

Let's see . . . that gives me 'til 3:30 this afternoon

to do some of my own Christmas shopping. The weather's still nice—a bit *too* nice, if you ask me . . . think I'll ride my Western Flyer bike to the downtown shops and look around by myself.

So I'm off, E.D. . . . Only six more shopping days till Christmas, and if I don't make a dent in my Christmas list pretty soon, I may have to boycott the whole holiday. But doing my own Christmas shopping has gotta be different than shopping with the Greedy Gremlins, right?

— *Click!* —

Back again. Time: fifteen-hundred hours *or* three o'clock P.M.—depending on whether you want time by the twenty-four-hour day or the twelve-hour clock . . . and this is Drea Thomas reporting in, E.D.

When I got home, there was a message on our answering machine for me to call George. Wonder what he wants? Tried calling him back but his line was busy.

Ta-da! I did make a dent in my list of people to buy for . . . well, only a little dent, but at least I found a perfect gift for Kimberly: red plaid suspenders and a matching beret. I wanted to give them to her early, before she leaves to spend Christmas with her grandmother, who has a condo somewhere in the Pocono Mountains . . . hmm, a "condo in the Poconos"—sounds pretty cool to me.

I also got a couple of stocking stuffers for Matt and Rebecca and a chew bone for Floyd, their overgrown shag rug with paws—ya know, the sheepdog who "redecorated" our dining room the weekend I baby-sat the Long kids . . . never mind. That's past history.

Anyway. Matt and Rebecca will be here soon. Maybe they'd like to help me decorate my bedroom for the holidays . . . oh! Speaking of "decking the halls," I got a cool idea while I was downtown. Some of the store windows had some really creative holiday scenes in 'em—ya know, Santa's workshop with busy little elves . . . Dicken's *A Christmas Carol*, with a miniature Scrooge dancing around with Tiny Tim on his shoulders . . .

And then there was one with a very simple manger scene. Shepherds and sheep and wise men and camels and a donkey all crowded around the baby Jesus sleeping in the manger, while Joseph and Mary stood by looking holy. But . . . there was something that didn't seem quite right about it. And then I realized what it was: there are still six days 'til Christmas, and already the baby Jesus was lying in the manger. Now if *I* were the window designer . . .

"No, no, no," I said to my window assistant, peering through horn-rimmed glasses at the manger scene he'd just set up. "A manger scene—yes! A

manger scene where all the characters are just standing there glassy-eyed for four weeks—no! We're competing with store windows full of snow bunnies dancing around Christmas trees and reindeer that fly!"

The assistant ran a hand over his buzz cut. "So?"

"SO," I said, whipping out my clipboard and jotting down some notes, "for starters we need three windows in a row . . ."

"Three windows!" The assistant acted like I was asking for the crown jewels of England.

"Yes . . . in the first one, here, we need to create the town of Bethlehem, complete with the Bethlehem Motel and a stable to park the traveler's vehicles—horses, donkeys, wagons—you get the picture. Street sellers hawking their wares! Kids running, dogs barking! In the background will be the surrounding countryside . . . flocks of sheep and good-hearted shepherds going about their duties."

The assistant rolled his eyes . . . but I was already in the second window. "Here we have Mary and Joseph with their donkey carrying all the luggage, making the long trek from Nazareth to Bethlehem—along with a zillion other disgruntled pilgrims forced to travel to their home towns on short notice by the Romans, who got the bright idea to count everybody in the known world."

"And the third window?" asked the assistant with bored patience.

"The wise men, of course!" I said, ideas spinning in my head. "They have the longest distance to travel. I want realistic-looking camels . . . and sandy desert . . . and wise men from different countries with richly-colored robes . . . and a dark velvet sky with a bright star that moves, until . . ."

"Until . . . ?"

"Do I hear an echo?" I eyed the assistant, then rushed back to the first window. "Then on Christmas Eve, alert window shoppers will see a new sight—a Jewish peasant family crowded into the stable with the animals next to a motel with a "No Vacancy" sign, and a brand-new baby sleeping in the feed trough."

My vision for an animated manger scene faded . . . but it gave me an idea, E.D.! So when I got home, I moved Mary and Joseph and the donkey out of our manger scene on the mantel and put them in the dining room, where they can travel closer and closer each day till Christmas . . . the shepherds and sheep are now "keeping watch" on the piano in the music room . . . and the wise men are traveling the farthest distance from the attic stairs. Finally I hid baby Jesus until it's time for Him to be "born" . . . Christmas Eve.

Oops. I hear the Long kids coming in the back door . . . catch ya later, E.D. Now I just wish I could get an idea that would solve the rest of my shopping problems. Still no idea for gifts for my family . . . and time is short!

— Click! —

Same day . . . same place . . . but it's now twenty-hundred hours and I've got the house to myself again . . . well, me and the mouse that I saw dart into the attic when I came up to my room a few minutes ago. But I'm excited, E.D. . . . I think I came up with an idea that's going to solve all our shopping problems!

But let me back up a couple hours.

When Matt and Rebecca arrived, I got out the box of leftover Christmas decorations and asked if they wanted to help me decorate my room. They mumbled, "Yeah, okay," and helped me put the extra strings of Christmas lights around the edge of the ceiling in my room, but then they got distracted by a bunch of magazines or something they'd brought along.

I dug around in the box of decorations, found some figures from "The Nutcracker Suite," and said, "Come on, guys, we haven't finished decorating."

"We're busy," Matt mumbled.

I put the Nutcracker himself on my bookcase, along with some Christmas tree balls and candy canes, but it didn't really look right . . .

"Maybe a little to the left," I suggested.

The wooden Nutcracker, in his spiffy blue and red uniform, stepped smartly to the left.

"No, that's too far," I said, eyeing the shelf critically. "Come back to the right . . . "

The Nutcracker took a giant step to the right.

"That's better . . . now, just a little forward . . ."

The Nutcracker stepped forward.

"That's great," I said. "Perfect . . ."

But the Nutcracker kept marching forward . . . left, right, left, right . . . until he fell right off the shelf!

"Hmmm," I said out loud to myself, picking up the Nutcracker and a smashed candy cane, "I just invented a 'Nutcracker Sweet.' "

Out of the corner of my eye, I saw Rebecca roll her eyes at my VBJ . . . Very Bad Joke. "Oh, well," I said, "decking the halls is still one of the most fun things about Christmas."

"*NOT!*" came a chorus behind me. I turned and saw that Matt and Rebecca were looking through some Christmas catalogs.

"What are you guys doing, anyway?" I asked, going over to the little table and peeking over their shoulders.

Matt marked something with a yellow highlighter.

"Just some last minute gift ideas," Rebecca said.

"Oh?" I said. "For whom?"

"For me!" Matt said . . . and was immediately poked by his sister. "Oh, yeah . . . and Rebecca, too," he added.

I rolled my eyes. The Greedy Gremlins were still at it.

Just then we heard Mrs. Long calling up the stairs, "Come on down, kids—it's time to go home."

As Matt and Rebecca gathered up their catalogs, Matt said, "Do you think it's too late to order this stuff?"

"It *says* they deliver by Christmas," Rebecca said hopefully, "but we'd need a credit card."

As their mother's voice called them again, their faces lit up. Ah-ha, a credit card source.

"Oh, Mo-om . . .!" they chorused sweetly and clattered down the stairs.

I followed them downstairs to the kitchen, where Mrs. Long was talking to Grandpa, who was sitting at the kitchen table with a cup of coffee and a crossword puzzle from the newspaper.

"Oh, hi, Grandpa," I said, giving him a kiss on top of his head. "I didn't know you were here."

"Oh, I just came by in case you were having something interesting for dinner . . . but things look pretty quiet in the Thomas kitchen tonight—that is, until the Dynamic Duo came clattering down the stairs."

The so-called Dynamic Duo were shoving catalogs in their mother's face. "Mom!" said Matt. "There's some cool stuff I want in here. What's your credit card number?"

"Yeah, we highlighted the order numbers to make it easy for you," Rebecca added helpfully.

Mrs. Long sighed. "Come on . . . we can talk about it in the car." As the kids ran out the back door, she turned back to me and Grandpa with an apologetic shrug. "My kids are turning into turbocharged shopping machines."

I had to agree with her there. "They're in high gear for gift-getting, that's for sure."

Mrs. Long hesitated, then said, "Trouble is . . .

the car was just in the shop, and yesterday the hot water heater went on the fritz. There's no way I can afford half of what they're asking for."

I didn't really know what to say, so I just said, "I'm sorry" and "Good luck" as she went out to her car.

Grandpa rubbed his chin thoughtfully. "She's right, ya know. Ever since the stores started advertising Christmas gifts right after Labor Day, it seems everybody focuses on *quantity*, not quality. Most people seem to have forgotten what Christmas is all about."

I slumped into a kitchen chair. "I can't even get the quantity part down. I feel like a total shopping disaster this year."

"Me, too," said my dad's voice. I looked up as Mom and Dad both came in from the hallway.

"Me three," said Mom. "I've been so busy with holiday campaigns for the store, I haven't had a chance to do anything for you guys." She looked around at all of us. "Maybe . . . maybe we should do something different this year."

My dad got a blank look. "Like what?" And that's when I got The Idea, E.D. . . . .

A Christmas tree light bulb seemed to go off in my brain, casting a rosy glow on the kitchen table.

I mean, if *quantity* is getting in the way of *quality* when it comes to gift giving, then . . .

"Hey, I've got an idea!" I said. "What if everyone just has to get one gift? We'll put all our names in a hat and each pick one."

I could almost see little Christmas light bulbs turning on over their heads as first Dad . . . then Mom . . . then Grandpa began to smile. The idea sank in.

"Well, that certainly would simplify things," Mom said enthusiastically. "I'll get some paper."

Dad rubbed his hands together like a kid in a candy store. "Okay, let's give it a shot."

Mom handed out pieces of paper and we each wrote our own name on one, then put them all into

Grandpa's baseball cap which he pulled off his head for the cause.

"Now, we can't tell each other whose name we've drawn," said Grandpa. "It'll be our Christmas morning surprise."

"*And* if you pick yourself, you gotta put it back," I added, giving my dad a warning look.

Dad raised his eyebrows innocently in a Who-Me? look.

"Should we set a price limit?" Mom asked. Good ol' Mom. You'd think she was the marketing director of a large department store or something.

I shook my head. "No . . . but it has to be a gift from the heart."

The grin on Grandpa's face widened. "I get it . . . somethin' extra special."

By now Dad's bushy eyebrows were wiggling up and down with excitement. "Okay . . . let's pick!"

Everybody drew a piece of paper out of Grandpa's cap. I saw Dad slyly try to peek at the name on Mom's paper before she caught him. "Hey! No cheating!" she said, pulling her paper away.

"Fine," Dad said, dramatically stuffing his piece of paper down the front of his shirt. "Two can play at that game." He strode to the back door, like a king in suspenders preparing for battle. "*I'm* going shopping."

"Me, too," said Mom, right on his heels. "Stores

are open to midnight." And just like that, they were gone.

Grandpa retrieved his cap and pushed his chair away from the kitchen table. "Guess I'll be going, too," he said, giving me a kiss good-bye. He grinned. "This is going to be fun."

He was gone before I realized he'd not only given me a kiss, but his empty coffee cup as well.

As I put the coffee cup in the sink, I looked at the kitchen clock: 6:15. "Hey, guys!" I started to call after them. "What about dinner?" But they were gone. Oh, well. They're big people. Guess they'll figure out they haven't eaten yet.

I leaned against the kitchen counter and looked at the name I had picked again. Grandpa was right. "This is going to be great," I said out loud.

Just then a gravelly toaster voice interrupted my thoughts. "So, Drea . . . who'd ya get? Who'd ya get?" It was the Prince of Pop Tarts, jumping up and down with curiosity.

I pulled my piece of paper out of snooping range. "I can't tell you," I said. "It's supposed to be a secret."

"Hey," said the toaster. "I won't tell a soul— promise. Small appliances are very trustworthy, you know. We even come with life-time guarantees!"

Mr. Toaster shot an official-looking document out of his slots, which then unrolled on the counter and hung down almost to the floor. The words across the top boldly proclaimed "Life-Time Guarantee."

"Sorry, Toaster," I shrugged. "Too much fine print."

He then muttered, "Humph, see if I ever share my secret for perfectly toasted English muffins."

"Must be a real secret," I teased him, "since I have yet to see a 'perfectly toasted' anything from YOU."

But talking about food, E.D., reminded me that it *was* dinner time, so I zapped a couple of slices of frozen pizza, made myself a "Christmas shake" — ice cream, milk, and candy cane chips—and brought it up here to my room to think. I'm talking major brain drain: I want to do something really special for my Secret Person for Christmas.

Sorry, E.D. . . . I can't even tell *you* who it is.

— *Click!* —

Later. Bedtime. Just saw the mouse again. I'm gonna name him Morton.

— *Click!* —

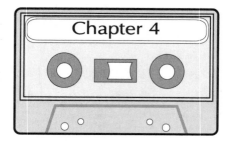

A One-Ski, No-Snow Day

G'morning, E.D. Drea Thomas, here, checking in with five days to go 'til Christmas.

Mom and Dad are so busy, they haven't noticed yet that the main characters are missing from the manager scene on the mantle. But I decided to move Mary and Joseph from the dining room to the doorway anyway, and I also moved the Wise Men down a few stairs.

On the plus side, everyone's really jazzed about my gift exchange idea, but now comes the tough part. When you only have one gift to give, it's sooo important to find just the right thing. Frankly, I wonder how much easier this is going to be?

I'm still giftless, so I called in professional help. Kimberly's gonna take me to her favorite stores downtown. But . . . I don't know if my folks are prepared for gifts from stores called Bell Bottom Dreams or Catastrophe.

Oh well. I'm supposed to meet Kimberly by thirteen-hundred-hours at Frankie's Fifties Cafe—that's the new hangout downtown, complete with a genuine Verlitzer jukebox! Dad says it's a classic. Anyway . . . it's almost twelve-thirty, so I'm outta here. Guess I'll ride my Western Flyer—got my own fifties classic, ya know. It'll feel right at home in the bike rack in front of Frankie's.

Over and out.

— Click! —

You will *not* believe this, E.D.! I feel kinda bad about what happened, but . . . when I think about it, I start laughing all over again!

Okay, okay, I'll start from the beginning. After getting a strawberry malt at Frankie's—can't shop on an empty stomach, ya know—we hit the stores. But by the time Kimberly and I came out of Stockton's—a housewares store for Yuppies—she

was getting pretty frustrated with me.

"Come on, Drea," she said. "That's the third store we've been in, and you haven't bought a single gift."

"I know," I said, staring in the window at the cappuchino coffee makers and the latest in copper-bottomed pots and pans, "but everything's so ordinary. I need something really special."

Maybe it was the twinkling lights around the window, or maybe it was my imagination working overtime, but . . .

One of the frying pans hanging at the back of the window display jumped off its hook, hit a big soup pot on its way down—"Ouch!" grunted the soup pot—did a double somersault, then hopped on its handle right up to the window. I wanted to

laugh, because it had a face like a puppy in a pet shop.

Then . . . it winked at me! What a flirt!

I smiled at the pan. "And everything that looks interesting," I admitted, "I don't know who I would give it to."

At this, the pan's puppy-dog face drooped, and it started to slowly hop away on its handle.

"Sorry, fella," I said . . .

44

"Oh, that's okay," a voice said behind me. "You really shoulda returned my phone call, but . . . I'll forgive ya."

I whirled around. "George!" I said, embarrassed that I'd been caught talking to myself . . . I mean, to a frying pan. George Easton was grinning that wonderful, lop-sided smile of his, wearing his usual jeans and flannel shirt.

"George, I'm sorry I didn't call you back," I blurted. "I tried once, but the line was busy . . . and I've been mondo busy since school let out."

"That's okay." George gave a little shrug. "I just wanted to tell you that I'm going to Florida for the holidays."

"You're going away, too?" said Kimberly. "When do you leave?"

"This afternoon," said George. "You know, it's 'off to Grandmother's house I go' . . ."

I suddenly realized this was going to be a lonesome Christmas vacation without both Kimberly *and* George.

"Well, Merry Christmas, George," I said, and on impulse I gave him a big hug. I mean . . . well, it *is* Christmas, E.D.

"You, too," he said, grinning. "Say, I'm heading for the Antique Store. You guys wanna come?"

Kimberly and I looked at each other and grimaced. "Been there . . . done that," we chorused.

"Okay," he said. "Gotta cruise. See ya next year."

I watched as George disappeared into the crowd of shoppers . . . then heard *another* voice behind me.

"Ahh. Another man racing away from you as fast as he can," said a sarcastic voice. "But you must be used to that by now."

Kimberly and I turned around slowly, coming face to face with—you guessed it, E.D.—Arlene Blake and Marcy Mannington.

I steadied my nerves. "Merry Christmas, Arlene," I said, trying to give Arlene a teensy-weensy hint that it *was* the season of good cheer and brotherly love.

Kimberly poked me and tipped her head in their direction. They made a comical pair: Arlene, dressed in cream-colored pants and matching cardigan sweater, was carrying one, small, dainty gift bag, while once again Marcy looked like a frazzled pack horse, carrying all sorts of packages and ski equipment.

Kimberly and I looked at each other. *Ski equipment?!*

"You know, Arlene, I hate to tell you this," Kimberly said, stifling a grin, "but in case you hadn't noticed . . . there's no snow."

"Very amusing, Andow," Arlene said with exaggerated patience. "This is my new ski package for my vacation in Aspen."

"Ya know . . . Aspen?" Marcy piped up. "That's in Colorado."

Honestly, E.D. As if we'd never heard of the most prestigious ski resort in the U.S. of A.

"I hope you have a nice time baby-sitting those bratty little Long kids while I'm mingling with the celebrities on the slopes," Arlene added, rubbing it in.

My mind was busy trying to think of a smart comeback, when I noticed something odd about Arlene's "ski package."

"Uh . . . Arlene," I said, "don't you think you'd have a better time with *two* skis?"

Arlene whirled on Marcy and saw that, sure enough, along with ski boots, poles, and other assorted bags from Sasha's Ski Shoppe, Marcy was carrying only one ski.

"Where's my other ski?" Arlene fumed at Marcy.

Marcy looked confused. "I don't know . . . we musta left it at the dry cleaners."

"*We*?!" Arlene snapped back. "You're the one who was carrying the skis. . . . So don't just stand there! Go get it!"

Kimberly and I watched Marcy unload all Arlene's stuff onto Arlene and run down the street. Kimberly poked me and snickered. Arlene *did* look pretty funny trying to manage ski, poles, boots, dry cleaning, and packages all at once without her trusty shadow.

Arlene was annoyed . . . big time. "What are you two staring at?" she snapped at us. Then she shrugged like a movie star brushing off pesky groupies. "Soooo immature."

We took the hint and started across the street.

"She hates you, you know," Kimberly said—as if I didn't know it—then warned, "Hey . . . watch out for the puddle."

A wide, muddy puddle stood between the curb and the street—the result of several recent downpours which *would* have been a great snowfall if it'd been thirty degrees instead of sixty.

We jumped over the puddle and dashed across the street to the shops on the other side.

"I know she hates me," I admitted, "but what did I ever do to her?"

Kimberly held up her hand and ticked off on her fingers, "You mean, *besides* stealing the town's best baby-sitting gig, humiliating her in the school election, convincing her rich grandfather to save the school's extracurricular activities, and—"

"Okay, okay, okay," I admitted, "a few, tiny, potentially embarrassing things, but—"

A loud blast on a horn drowned out any attempt at conversation. We whipped around to see a delivery van swerving to avoid a car crowding the center line. A wall of water erupted with a humongous *WHOOSH!* as the van sped through the puddle next to the curb.

As the van disappeared down the street, my mouth dropped open. Arlene—perfect, spotless

Arlene Blake, the girl who cares about her looks more than anything—was covered from head to foot with muddy ooze.

"Ooooo . . . yuck!" she shrieked, stomping her foot. Furious, she dropped the muddy ski, poles, boots, and packages and tried to wipe mud out of her eyes with an equally grimy hand.

Sorry, E.D., the temptation to laugh was *so* great. I really couldn't blame Kimberly for cracking up.

"Stop it!" screeched Arlene. "*Stop laughing!*"

I stifled the urge to giggle and instead called across the street, "Arlene, are you okay?"

Just then George came up the sidewalk—back from the Antique Store I guess—and stopped dead in his tracks. "Whoa . . . what happened?" he said, genuinely concerned. "Ahh, Arlene, can I help you? Hose you off or something?"

Arlene looked like she was about to throw a temper tantrum, right then and there.

"No—thank—you!" she spit out between clenched teeth.

George looked over at us, shrugged, then disappeared into the crowd of holiday shoppers.

I was debating whether to go back across the street and see if we could help Arlene, when Marcy came back with the other ski. She gaped at Arlene, then quickly tried to collect the muddy packages. But Arlene yelled at her—especially when Marcy picked up a dirty ski boot and accidently poured more muddy water down Arlene's now mud-colored wool pants.

"This is all your fault, Drea Thomas!" Arlene screamed at me across the street.

I looked at Kimberly, astonished. "*Me?!* What did I do?"

Kimberly rolled her eyes. "Nothing . . . Arlene just got her ego covered with mud, and she needs to blame somebody. Come on." She grabbed my arm and pulled me down the sidewalk. "I know this stuff . . . believe me. I watch Oprah Winfrey."

Oh, right, I thought. As if a TV talk show host from Chicago could possibly know why Arlene Blake hates me. As Kimberly steered me toward another store, I looked back over my shoulder. Arlene was yelling something after me, but I couldn't hear what.

But I have an uncomfortable feeling I'm going to find out.

— Click! —

Still Tuesday, E.D. . . . Mom and Dad both worked late again, so we went out for pizza when they got home. We invited Grandpa, who was puttering around at his workbench in our garage, but he yelled through the door that he was "busy" and told us all to stay out.

When we got home, Kimberly had left a message for me on our answering machine . . . here, I'll run it again and you can hear it for yourself, E.D. . . .

Bleep. Whirrrrrrrrrrr . . . Bleep.

Drea? This is Kimberly. I don't know if Arlene is bluffing or what, but . . . I ran into Cristan Canter and she'd been talking to Lauren who knows Marcy who said that Arlene Blake is vowing to make this your most miserable Christmas ever. Like I told you, Drea . . . the girl has a PROBLEM! Anyway, talk to ya later . . .

Bleep.

So. What do you think of that, E.D.? For some reason Arlene thinks that if she and Marcy hadn't stopped to talk to me and Kimberly, this whole mud incident never would have happened.

Oh, brother. Now I'm back on Arlene's black list . . . or at least her muddy brown list. This could put a major *SNAG* in my Christmas vacation. Lucky Kimberly . . . she's leaving town.

Sigh. I *was* dreaming of a white Christmas, E.D. . . . right now, I'd settle for a *right* Christmas—but that's all it is, I guess . . . a dream.

— Click! —

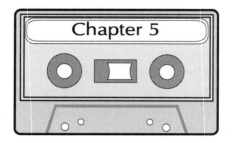

Chapter 5

Surfin' Santa's Comin' to Town

Day 4,942 in the Secret Adventures of Drea Thomas . . . and something very weird is goin' on, E.D.

When I came downstairs for breakfast this morning, Dad was on the kitchen phone.

"No," he was saying, "that's what I'm trying to tell you. We're not moving."

My heart did two and a half flip-flops. *Moving?* Who was talking about moving?

Just then Mom walked in, dressed for work, wearing a pretty, navy suit with white trim. "Hi, everybody," she said, pouring herself a cup of coffee. "Did you say someone's moving?"

Dad ran his hand through his hair, making it

stand up like that guy who plays Doc Brown in *Back to the Future*. "Someone thinks *we* are," he said. "That's the third call this morning from someone wanting to buy our house!"

Mom took another hurried swig of her coffee. "Hmm," she said. "What were they offering?"

Dad gave her an exasperated look. "I didn't ask! Laurie . . . I love this house. I don't want to move."

Just then the phone rang *again*.

Dad groaned. "It's your turn," he said to Mom. "I've had it with the real estate boom."

Frankly, E.D., I was totally confused.

"Hello?" Mom said. ". . . No, I'm sorry, there must be some mistake . . . *how much?*"

Dad and I both glared at her.

". . . No, no, that's okay," she said hastily. "We're not selling."

As Mom hung up the phone, Grandpa came in the back door. This was kinda early for him—he often hangs out at our house, but not usually at eight in the morning. On the other hand, he's been spending a lot of time locked in the garage the last couple of days . . .

Anyway. When he came in, he was holding a stake with a FOR SALE sign nailed to it . . . with our phone number printed in bold type at the bottom!

"This was stuck in the front yard," he said, looking sternly at Dad, then at Mom and me. "How much do you want for the place? Maybe I'll buy it."

Dad threw up his hands. "Well! That explains all the phone calls."

"You mean you're not selling?" said Grandpa, a relieved smile cracking his face. "Heh, heh . . . 'course I suspected all along you wouldn't move without telling me."

"Of course not, Grandpa," I said, giving him a hug. "I don't know anything about it, either."

"Hmmm," Mom said, "do you suppose there's a crazy real estate agent on the loose in our neighborhood? You know, sticking up FOR SALE signs to get people to think about selling?"

Dad shook his head. "Probably somebody's idea of a joke. The best thing to do is just take the sign down and move on . . . or not move on, as the case may be."

"Good idea," said Mom, slugging down the last of her coffee and grabbing a yogurt from the refrigerator. "Gotta run . . . only four days till Christmas, you know, and the marketing department at Jamison's is already gearing up for the January sales."

Dad held out a thumb. "Going my way?"

Mom pointed a finger at him. "Bing Crosby! 1944!"

Dad stared at her blankly. "Huh?"

"Let's go," she grinned, "I'll explain it in the car."

As the door closed behind my parents, Grandpa

shook his head and hummed a few bars of a tune that sounded vaguely familiar . . . like some show tune from an old musical. "Tum-de-dum, tum-de-dum-dum . . . 'Going My Way'—great Bing Crosby movie," he said, his eyes kinda dreamy. "Ahh, Drea, those were the days when they made *real* movies . . . without all this cussing and violence you see today."

"Grandpa!" I said impatiently. "This isn't the time to talk about old movies. Someone just tried to sell our house out from under us!"

Grandpa biffed me on the nose. "Hey, don't worry. Your house just went off the market . . . and *I* gotta work on my gift for my Secret Person." With that, Grandpa shoved the FOR SALE sign in my hands and was out the door.

Exactly one second later it swung open again and Grandpa poked his head back in. "Just remember . . . the garage is *off limits*." And his head disappeared again.

Whew. I'd only been in the kitchen ten minutes, and already I felt like I'd been through a time warp. One minute the whole family was standing in the kitchen taking calls from perfect strangers who wanted to buy our house . . . and the next moment, I was left alone to scrounge my own breakfast. I tossed the FOR SALE sign in the garbage can, stuck my head in the refrigerator and muttered, "I think everyone around here has lost their mind . . ."

"So what else is new?" said a gravelly voice. "I thought that was a genetic trait of the Thomases."

Correction. Alone in the house with a talking toaster.

"Good morning, Toaster," I said, greeting the heap of shiny chrome and heating elements that make up my friend, Mr. Toaster. "Guess you heard about the FOR SALE sign that just appeared on our lawn."

"Uh-huh," said the toaster, "and I've got an idea about the sign bandit." One of Mister Toaster's handles morphed into a magnifying glass, which he peered into intently.

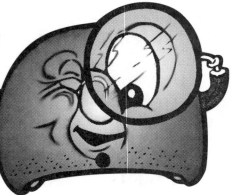

"Were there any MUDDY SKI BOOTS at the scene of the crime, eh?"

"Muddy ski boots? You mean . . . nahhh. Arlene wouldn't do something so crazy . . . would she?" I shook the thought out of my mind.

"Well, look, Toaster," I said, starting to leave with a glass of juice in my hand, "I've got things to do, gifts to buy . . ."

"That's the one for your mom, right?" said the toaster casually.

I started to answer him—then caught myself just in time. "Nice try, Toaster," I said. "But I'm still not revealing my Secret Person."

I tell you, E.D., it's hard to keep a secret around here. That's why I'm not even telling *you* whose name I drew for Christmas. I wouldn't put it past my family to accidentally punch the "play" button on this Walkman . . .

Anyway, Kimberly's going to her Grandma's today and I want to give her my Christmas gift before she leaves. Time: oh-nine-hundred hours . . . temperature: a mild fifty-five degrees—which means my jeans and a sweatshirt oughta be okay for bike riding . . . and I'm outta—

Riiiiiinnnnnnnnggg.

Of course! The phone! Happy holidays, Miss L. Toe speaking . . .

— *Click!* —

I gotta be careful how I answer the phone, E.D. That was Mrs. Long—who is not only the junior high principal, but my baby-sitting employer. Not sure what she thought of my "mistletoe" joke. Anyway . . . she wanted to know if I can baby-sit Matt and Rebecca tomorrow evening—including dinner. Told her it would be okay . . . she sounded kinda down. It must be tough to be a single mom, especially around the holidays . . .

Anyway, as I was saying before the phone rang . . . I'm outta here.

— Click! —

This is too much, E.D.! First the FOR SALE sign, now this . . . but wait, I'm getting ahead of myself again.

It's still Day 4,942 . . . Time: fifteen-hundred hours—that's three o'clock in New Jersey . . . Place: up in my bedroom where I can think out loud . . . because, as I said before, something very weird is going on around here.

This morning I rode over to Kimberly's house on my Western Flyer, and she really liked the red plaid suspenders and matching beret I got her at Flashions. They'll look great with her long dark hair.

I told Kimberly about the FOR SALE sign appearing in front of our house this morning, and she about had heart failure. She's *sure* Arlene Blake is behind it. She immediately wanted to help me plot "Drea's Revenge," but I told her to forget it. Right then I was more concerned about finding the right gift for my special person. I didn't have time to worry about Arlene.

Anyway. After the Andows took off, I did some more "window shopping." Got a couple crazy ideas, like the wax hand where each finger was really a candle . . . thought it might come in handy the next time my Special Person says, "Give me a hand, will ya, Drea?" And I really laughed at the T-shirt that said, "Bad Spellers of the World—UNTIE!" . . . except no one in my family is a bad speller. Then there was the display for a jazzy, new alarm clock that promised, "Tired of waking up to the same old jarring jangle? Wake up instead to the sounds of nature!" I wondered what "sounds of nature" the ad was talking about . . . birds twittering? a brook babbling? My imagination began sorting through the possibilities . . .

The store display faded momentarily as I saw myself snoring gently in my bed with the new, glow-in-the-dark alarm clock on my night stand gently ticking toward the wake-up hour. Then suddenly I bolted upright in bed, cracking my head on the slanted roof of my attic room, as the alarm clock let loose with an earsplitting "sound of nature"—a shrill COCK-A-DOODLE-DOOOOOOOOOO!

I winced and decided not to take a chance on the alarm clock, either . . . and finally rode my bike home, thinking about my "one gift" idea. It's not as easy as I thought. As I came up the driveway, Dad was already home shooting baskets—short day at the college, I guess.

"Hey, Drea!" he huffed, dribbling the ball, "how 'bout a little one-on-one? I just got home myself."

Normally I really like to play basketball with Dad. He put up the basketball hoop when we first moved into this house, and would let me stand on his shoulders to throw the basketball in. But today I really wasn't in the mood for basketball.

"Sorry, Dad," I said, swinging off my Western Flyer. "I'm beat . . . and I've got stuff to do."

"Oh. Well, at least you don't have as much shopping to do," he said. "I think your 'one gift' idea is really great."

I shrugged. "Yeah, maybe . . . if you can find one gift that shows everything you feel about one of the most important people in your life."

Dad stopped dribbling and put the basketball on his hip. "Whoa," he said. "When you put it like that, it kinda puts the pressure on, doesn't it?"

I nodded, discouraged.

But Dad doesn't give up easily. "Come on," he urged, throwing me the ball, "take your mind off your troubles. Take a shot."

So I decided to give it one shot, just to humor

him. But just to show I didn't really care, I turned my back to the basket and threw the basketball over my head.

You will never believe this, E.D. That ball seemed to travel in slow motion . . . up . . . up . . . up . . . then down . . . down . . . down . . . and *swhoosh!*— right into the basket.

Dad's eyes nearly popped out of his head as he caught the ball underneath the net.

"*YES!*" I said, giving it the ol' one-two elbow tucks.

Dad walked over to me, basketball under his arm, running a hand through his hair. "Hey," he grumbled, "are you trying to make your old man look bad?" Then a slow grin spread over his face as he held up his hand and slapped me a high five. "Nice shootin', kid," he said proudly, as we headed for the house.

But when we came in the back door, we could hardly get into the kitchen. The entire room was filled with huge packing boxes . . . and when I say huge, E.D., I mean the size of kitchen stoves!

Dad's jaw dropped. "What *is* all this?" he said, backed up against the clothes dryer in the entryway.

Grandpa's voice came from somewhere near the refrigerator. "They came for Drea this afternoon," he said, coming up between a couple boxes with a soft drink in his hand. "Something for a fund-raiser you're doin', huh?"

I didn't answer. I was too shocked. Pushing my way into the kitchen between boxes, I fished in a drawer for some scissors while Dad picked up a packing slip. " 'Thank you for your order,' " he read aloud. " 'Packing slip number fifteen of . . . thirty'?"

Grandpa leaned against a box and shrugged. "They came C.O.D. . . . but I paid for 'em," he said, looking pointedly in my direction. Then he handed Dad a slip of paper. "Here's the receipt."

Dad snatched the receipt, and then his eyes got very big. "One hundred and ninety-two dollars . . . ?" he said in a state of shock.

"*And* thirty-six cents," Grandpa pointed out.

Meanwhile I was digging in the box I'd opened and pulled out a foot-high Santa Claus doll . . . except this Santa Claus was wearing a brightly-colored Hawaiian shirt, swim trunks, and sandals, and was holding a florescent red-and-green surf board.

I looked at the doll, then at Grandpa and Dad. "Surfin' Santas?" I said, totally bewildered.

"Boy, I hope you got a discount for ordering so many," said Dad. Both he and Grandpa were looking at me in a we'd-like-to-be-supportive-but-are-you-crazy? kind of way.

"But," I protested, "I didn't order *any* of these stupid things!"

Grandpa's jaw dropped and we all stood there just staring at each other. Then, shaking their heads, he and Dad threaded their way through the boxes out of the kitchen, leaving me—somehow—holding Grandpa's empty soda can.

I almost called after them, "But I think I know who did"—except I don't really know, and before I go blaming Arlene for these stupid tricks, I better get some more evidence. In the meantime, E.D., I've got a more immediate problem: what to do with thirty boxes taking up every square inch in the kitchen, *and* how am I going to pay Grandpa back one hundred ninety-two dollars . . . and thirty-six cents?

— Click! —

Dear E.D. . . . I was up in my room after dinner when I heard Dad yelling, "Those tricksters have struck again!"

I rushed downstairs to find Dad standing in the living room, his face bright red, and pointing at the empty manger scene on the mantle.

"This is the last straw!" he fumed. "Coming

right in our house and taking Mary and Joseph—"

"Uh, Dad," I interrupted, pulling on his sleeve. "I did it."

He looked at me blankly. "You? You put up the FOR SALE sign? And . . . those boxes? But I thought you said—"

"No, no," I said hastily. "I took the figures out of the manger scene." So I explained my idea about treating the manger scene more like a little play than a decoration, moving the figures closer each day, waiting 'til Christmas to put the baby Jesus in the manger . . . stuff like that.

Well, once he understood, he said it was a good idea. But . . . I don't think I should have waited for him to "discover" it. I think he just got five more gray hairs.

— Click! —

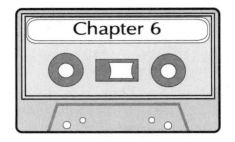

Jingle Bell, Jingle Bell, Jingle Bell *Shock*

Okay, E.D., I tried calling that Surfin' Santa company to tell them it's all a big mistake . . . oops. Almost forgot to date this entry. This is an electronic *diary*, after all . . .

Today is Day 4,943 in the Secret Adventures of Drea Thomas—only three days 'til Christmas. I don't have a gift yet for my Special Person—but I *do* have dozens of Surfin' Santas cluttering up the house. I tried stacking them in the corners and on top of the washer and dryer but Mom's still annoyed . . . she wants those boxes outta there! At least my parents and Grandpa *do* believe me that I didn't order the silly things, but still . . . the boxes *were* addressed to me, so I feel responsible to do something about them. But so far the toy company hasn't called me back—

Riiiiiinnnnnnnnggg.

Hey—maybe that's my call . . .

Toyland, home of the famous Surfin' Santa . . . what? Yes, this is Drea Thomas . . . I volunteered to do *what?*

— Click! —

Oh, noooo, E.D.! What am I gonna do now? That wasn't the toy company . . . it was somebody named Lieutenant Pierce from the Salvation Army calling. She thinks I volunteered to work for them tomorrow, and she says they're desperate! I don't believe this!

— Click! —

Okay, E.D., I took a little time to calm down and think this through. This is what happened.

The lady on the phone—Lieutenant Pierce—was actually very nice. She said, "We're so happy you called to volunteer. We feel so encouraged when young people want to help those less fortunate than themselves—"

"But . . . I didn't volunteer," I interrupted.

It was the Salvation Army lady's turn to be confused. "Didn't volunteer?" she said. "Is this Drea Thomas at . . ." and she read our address over the phone.

"Yes, but—"

"Then we received a call from you, volunteering a day of your time to work before Christmas—and it couldn't have come at a better time, because one of our volunteers is sick and . . ."

At this point, E.D., I panicked, trying to imagine myself ringing one of those Salvation Army bells all day. I mean, I was in jingle bell shock!

It took quite a while, but I finally convinced her that I hadn't called them, that *someone* was playing a joke on me.

"But," she said, "couldn't you consider volunteering anyway? We really are desperate for volunteers at this time of year in our store . . ."

That made me blink. "Store?" I asked. "What store? I thought you needed a volunteer to ring one of your bells—you know, for donations to the Salvation Army."

"Oh, no!" she laughed. "We have plenty of volunteer bell-ringers. No, I'm talking about volunteers to staff our second-hand store. It's especially important this time of year, because for some people, our store is the only way they can afford to buy Christmas gifts. But . . . one of our Christmas volunteers got sick with the flu, and we have no one for tomorrow to keep things straightened up and help customers. That's why we were so delighted when we got your call—"

"But I didn't call," I reminded her.

"Well, when we got your name and number then," she corrected herself. "Anyway, we only need someone for six hours tomorrow, from ten to four . . . would you consider doing it anyway? It would be a big help!"

It was all happening so fast, I really needed time to think! So I finally told her I would call her back.

But . . . I don't know what to do, E.D.! It's not that I mind helping out the Salvation Army. It's just that I still haven't decided what to give the person whose name I drew for Christmas . . . *and* I have to baby-sit Matt and Rebecca tonight . . . so if I give away my time tomorrow, that would leave only one day to get my act together!

Besides . . . if Arlene Blake is behind this, I would *hate* to give her the satisfaction of knowing that she really put a *SNAG* in my Christmas plans—

Oh, hi, Morton . . .

It's that cute little mouse, E.D. He must have a hole into my room somewhere . . . *sigh*. He seems so calm and peaceful . . . why can't I be calm and peaceful like that? Here it is Christmas—the most wonderful time of the whole year—and I don't know if I'm comin' or goin'! Christmas is supposed to be about sharing the greatest love in the world— God's Son coming to live among ordinary people— but . . . everything's gotten all mixed up with giving and getting and—

Maybe I should go talk to Grandpa—that is, if

he'll let me in the garage . . . hey, wait a minute. What was that verse he quoted a couple days ago when we were decorating? Something about "loving not in words, but in action"? Hmmmm . . .

— Click! —

Okay, E.D., I took some time to think about this, and I've decided what to do. I'm gonna go ahead and volunteer at the Salvation Army store. Don't ask me to explain it, 'cause there are a lot of reasons why it doesn't make sense . . . but I also have a feeling it just might have something to do with having a "right" Christmas . . .

— Click! —

Back again, E.D. It's now nineteen-hundred hours, and we just finished dinner and the dishes. Matt and Rebecca are up in my room . . . they've been sulking ever since they arrived, and I don't know why.

But I want to report that one problem seems to have been resolved. The sales manager of the Surfin' Santa company *finally* called me back just now as Mom and I were finishing up the dishes.

"Well?" Mom asked as I hung up the phone.

"The company said they'll issue a refund check and pick up the Santas after Christmas," I said—and boy, was I relieved. Now Grandpa would get his money back.

But Mom was hung up on that teensy-weensy lil' phrase, "after Christmas."

"Great," she said, shoving a box aside with her hip. "Did they have any suggestions about what we're supposed to do with them until then?"

"I'm sorry, Mom," I said. "I'll put 'em in the garage as soon as Matt and Rebecca leave."

Mom threw a dish towel over her shoulder and looked at me sideways. "Honey . . . these practical jokes are getting out of hand. Do you have any idea who's behind them?"

"Maybe," I hedged, "but I don't have any real proof. Besides, what could I say to someone who's committed to ruining my Christmas?"

Mom put a hand on her hip and narrowed her eyes. "How about, 'Knock it off, or I'm gonna sic my Mom on you.' "

Which is precisely the reason I haven't told Mom and Dad about this whole stupid thing with Arlene, E.D. The last thing I need is for my mom to go calling up Arlene's mom . . . Arlene would never let me live it down!

But I had to laugh at Mom's menacing look. "That's okay, Mom," I grinned. "I'll try to figure out something."

But frankly, E.D., I don't have a clue how to stop

Arlene. Let's just hope she's got it out of her system by now . . .

Guess I'll move Mary and Joseph to the windowsill near the fireplace, then go do something with Matt and Rebecca . . .

— Click! —

Time: twenty-two-hundred hours . . . and I just got done moving all those boxes to the garage. 'Course, just getting Grandpa's permission to get *into* the garage took the skills of a foreign diplomat. He's got some project going on in there, and he had to come over and cover it all up before he'd let me move the boxes in.

Now I'm ready for bed—gotta get some shut-eye before I enlist as a Salvation Army "soldier" tomorrow—but first, E.D., I want to tell you something that happened tonight with Matt and Rebecca.

After doing the dishes, I went upstairs to my room, but my mind was on this crazy business with Arlene *and* the fact that Christmas is only two days away and I still don't have a gift for my Special Person. When I opened the door, my room was dark except for some moonlight coming through the skylight . . . and then I saw this large, dark figure in front of my window!

"Aaaiiieeee!" I screamed and quickly flipped on the light.

Two faces jerked around . . . and I saw that the "large" figure was just Matt and Rebecca scrunched together on my window seat looking out the window into the mild, December sky.

"Sorry, Drea," Rebecca said, "it's just us."

"Oh, right," I said, feeling kinda silly for screaming. "What are you doing in the dark?"

"We wanted to make a wish on the Christmas star," Rebecca said seriously.

"But we couldn't find it," said Matt sadly.

I plopped down in my rocking chair, which was occupied by Stanley the Cat, one of my stuffed animals. "Maybe you'll see it Christmas Eve," I said, absently cuddling the stuffed Siamese cat. My mind was already back on more important problems.

"But that'll be too late," Matt said, sticking out his bottom lip. "You gotta see it before that for your Christmas Wish to come true." He slumped back on the cushions of the window seat. "It doesn't matter . . . our Christmas is ruined anyway."

That got my attention. "Huh?" I said. "Ruined? Why?"

Matt and Rebecca looked at each other and sighed.

"Well, we were shopping with Mom this morning," Rebecca explained, "and Matt wanted Mom to go into the toy store—"

"Yeah!" Matt interrupted. "I wanted to show her somethin' . . . but she said there was *no way* we were going to get Grandma 'florescent slime' for Christmas . . . but I don't know why not. Then I could play with it when I go to Grandma's house."

"I wanted to go into the toy store, too—just to see if there was anything new since you took us, Drea," Rebecca said. "But Mom got kinda mad and said it was time for a little talk. She sat us down on a bench and said we're supposed to be out shopping for other people—"

"But I told her I kept seeing things *I* want," Matt interrupted. "Then she gave us this long lecture about how tight money is this year . . ."

"So what I wanted to know was, what was she saying *exactly*?" Rebecca put in primly.

"She said we have to cut back on presents this year," Matt said, looking cross, "which really *stinks*, if you ask me."

This was becoming a major pity party—fast. "Hey," I said, "look at the bright side . . . at least your car is out of the shop and you guys have hot water again."

Matt gave me a disgusted look. "That's exactly what Mom said. What is this? A conspiracy to ruin my Christmas *and* make me take a bath?"

"Yeah, Drea," said Rebecca, "what good is Christmas without a lot of presents?"

"It's just not fair!" said Matt. "I've been good all year . . . for nothin'."

They were both so serious I wanted to burst out laughing. But just then we heard a squeaking sound . . . and Morton ran across my rug.

"Eeeeeeeeek!" screeched Rebecca, pulling her legs off the floor onto the window seat. "There's a mouse!"

"Don't worry," I grinned. "That's just Morton."

Which gave me an idea, E.D. I looked at Morton the mouse nosing his way around the edge of my room . . . then at Stanley, the stuffed cat in my lap. "Hmmm," I said aloud, "I wonder what Morton's got planned for Christmas."

Matt looked at me as if I was nuts. "Mouses don't have Christmases," he said with seven-year-old certainty.

"Sure they do," I insisted.

"Drea," Rebecca said, rolling her eyes, "come on."

I shrugged and wiggled Stanley the cat at them. "Guess I'll have to show you then. I just hope I can muster up enough imagination for a . . . Secret Adventure."

Matt and Rebecca looked at each other again— but this time the pouts on their faces slowly gave way to excited grins as the room began to spin and sparkle around us . . .

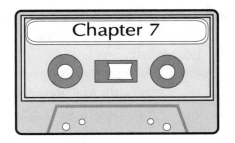

Chapter 7

All the Creatures Were Stirring, Even a Mouse

"Whoa, where are we?"

"Hey, Drea! Where'd you go?"

Two, small gray mice were looking around with puzzled expressions. The slightly larger one was wearing wire rim glasses and a red ski sweater, and the other a familiar blue baseball cap with a red brim.

"Here I am, guys," I said popping out from under a humongous floor pillow.

"Eeek! You're a mouse, Drea—a big brown one!" Rebecca screeched.

Matt and I looked at each other, then, laughing, pointed at Rebecca's pink ears and long tail.

"Yuk!" said Rebecca, peering through her glasses and giving her furry body a once-over. "I'm a MOUSE . . . and I hate mice."

"Why does everything look so—so big and strange, Drea?" Matt, the smallest gray mouse, squeaked, eyeing our surroundings timidly.

"Yeah, Drea," said Rebecca, sniffing the air with her stubby gray nose. "I mean, this place looks kinda familiar, but at the same time, everything looks so—so different."

I looked around, trying to be calm, cool, and collected—but frankly, I wasn't prepared either for how it felt to be the size of a tiny mouse. Kinda scary. I recognized my attic bedroom, all right—but on a gigantic scale. The rag rug on the floor looked like a multi-colored football field. The rocking chair and desk chair had legs like tree trunks. And the bed looked like a huge building, with a quilted "wall" hanging over the side and a large, open space where the "first floor" should have been.

"Hey—there's that red sock I've been missing!" I shouted, scurrying under the bed and nosing the large, red, cloth tube. "And here're my missing science notes . . . and, uh-oh, an overdue library book . . ."

Rebecca Mouse folded her front paws across her chest and tapped her hind paw. "Guess who needs to clean under her bed more often," she said.

"You mean . . . we're still in Drea's bedroom? But we've SHRUNK?" squeaked Matt Mouse.

"You got it, buddy," I said, diving out from under the bed and coming to a screeching halt in front of Matt and Rebecca. "How else are we going to be able to find Morton's mouse hole? C'mon . . . let's explore!"

I led the way across the rag rug and did a quick pass-through under my school desk. The bottom drawer was open, so we shinnied up the edge and dropped down inside.

"Ow . . . ooo . . . ick," Matt muttered. "These whiskers are so big they touch EVERYTHING."

"Guess that's how mice feel their way in the dark," I said, trying to maneuver my tail, which wasn't that easy—especially in a tight place.

"Boy, what a lot of junk you've got in here, Drea," said Rebecca in a muffled voice from under a massive array of old school papers, photos, dried-out markers, a jump rope, stickers, letters from Aunt Beth . . .

"Yeah, yeah, yeah, I'll clean it out one of these days," I said, sniffing a stale jelly bean that looked

as large as an eggplant—and about as appealing.
There were certain disadvantages to giving Miss
Super-Neat Rebecca Long a mouse-eye view of my
bedroom. "C'mon, let's keep going. This is a BIG
room . . ."

As we tumbled out of the desk drawer and stood
uncertainly on the rug by the rocking chair, we
heard a strange, rasping sound . . . from above.

I looked up. Looking down at me over the edge
of the rocking
chair seat was
Stanley, my
stuffed
Siamese
cat . . .
except
he was
very big,
very
much

alive, and looking at us with narrow, green eyes.

"What's the matter, Stanley?" I laughed nervously. "Don't you recognize me?"

Stanley's mouth opened in a wicked grin and he
licked his chops.

"Guess not," I muttered. I hadn't figured on
Stanley in this Secret Adventure. "Uh, kids," I said,
trying not to sound alarmed, "let's get out of here."

Rebecca took one look and screamed, "Run!"

Okay, so forget being calm, cool, and collected. Trying to get out of Stanley's reach, we shinnied up the legs of my desk chair and pulled ourselves onto the flat seat. But we'd hardly caught our breath when a pair of chocolate brown ears and green eyes poked up over the other side of the seat.

"Head for the steamer trunk!" I yelled. All three of us slid down the chair legs faster than Stanley could say, "Three Blind Mice," and made a beeline for the little hole in the corner of my grandmother's old trunk.

Zip . . . zip . . . zip. All three of us dived through the hole and crowded together, gasping for breath in the darkness. All I could see were two pairs of frightened mouse eyes.

The panting grew louder and heavier. "Oh, g—guys," said Matt's voice nervously. Slowly we all turned and looked behind us. Another pair of eyes . . . large, green eyes . . . were gleaming in the darkness.

"Aaaaaiiiiieeeeee!" Matt's voice screamed.

"Aaaaaiiiiieeeeee!" Rebecca's voice screamed.

"Aaaaaiiiiieeeeee!" I screamed . . . and the three of us shot around the inside of that steamer trunk like we had firecrackers tied to our tails. But everywhere we turned, those gleaming, green eyes were right behind us.

"Look out!" I yelled as the eyes closed in on Matt . . . or was it Rebecca? I didn't take time to find out, because the next moment we were going straight up the side of that steamer trunk so fast that the lid flew open, and we exploded like three rockets straight up into fresh air.

"Quick, I think Morton's hole is this way!" I yelled, landing with a triple somersault and taking off running toward the window seat and hoping that Matt and Rebecca were right behind me.

But as we neared our goal, Stanley leaped right in front of us. I could almost hear brakes screeching as Matt and Rebecca and I changed directions.

"Head for the stairs!" Rebecca yelled.

Under "normal" circumstances, the distance from the window seat to the three little stairs that lead to the landing in the corner of my room is a mere five or six steps. But when you're a mouse—even a mouse with four legs—it felt like the hundred-yard dash. But just when we thought we were going to cross the finish line, Stanley blocked our way AGAIN.

"Yikes!" yelled Matt. "We're trapped!"

It was true. With the bookshelves along the wall, we couldn't head that direction. The steamer trunk wasn't safe. We could run under the bed . . . but so could the cat.

He knew it, too. With a smug smile, Stanley smacked his mouth and gathered himself for the pounce . . .

"LOOK OUT BELOW!" yelled a strange voice . . . and the next thing we knew, a stack of books fell on top of Stanley's head. The cat just lay there, dazed, buried under Webster's dictionary, two Anne of Green Gables books—the hardcover editions—and a copy of The Joy of Cats.

Matt, Rebecca, and I looked up. There was my friend, Morton Mouse, standing on top of the bookcase, dressed in a crumpled top hat, a ragged black vest, and a red Christmas tie . . . and looking very pleased with himself.

"Cheerio!" he grinned, doffing the hat. I wanted to laugh. Someone once said the architecture of our house was sorta "Queen Anne"—maybe that's why Morton the house mouse spoke with a blimey English accent! "Is that what you're looking for?" he said, and tipped his hat toward a hole in the wall down behind my desk.

There it was! Morton's hole!

Just then I heard a bump and a thump. Stanley was recovering from the little jolt he'd experienced and was trying to crawl out from under the books.

"Okay, guys, let's go for it!" I said, taking off toward the hole. In went Matt . . . then Rebecca . . . then me . . . and bringing up the rear was Morton himself.

Whew! We were safe at last!

"Thanks for saving us, Morton," I said gratefully.

"It was mah pleasure, Miss," he said with a little bow. I had to admit, his manners and his accent were charming.

"Matt and Rebecca," I said, "I'd like you to meet a friend of mine, Mr. Morton Mouse . . ."

"Esquire," corrected Morton.

"Esquire," I added.

Morton bowed again. "Glad to make your acquaintance. Why, me and the family was just sitting down for a wee bit o' Christmas suppah when we heard the commotion out theah . . . won't ya join us?"

Matt and Rebecca looked puzzled as Morton led the way into another little room, decorated with bits of evergreen and red ribbon. Mrs. Morton, wearing a shawl and bonnet, and several mouse children— just the size of Matt Mouse and Rebecca Mouse— were sitting around a "table" which looked suspiciously like a discarded matchbox. Empty thread spools served as chairs, and the table was set with bottle caps, in which were small bits of bread and cheese.

"This here's me wife," said Morton proudly, "and the little 'uns—David . . . Diana . . . Jamison . . . and tiny Emma. All right, everybody," he said, clapping his paws, "make room for me new chums . . . Drea, Rebecca, and little Matt."

Matt Mouse screwed up his whiskers. "Little?" he protested.

There was good-natured shuffling as the mouse children buddied up to free up three spools for their guests.

"Oh, we couldn't impose," I hastened to say, noticing how little food there was on the table. "There's barely enough for your own family."

"Don't you be silly," said Morton, brushing away my concern. "There's always enough to share with friends. Now . . . let's have a prayer, if you please."

Morton took off his tattered top hat and shut his eyes. Matt, Rebecca, and I joined hands with the mice family and bowed our heads as Morton prayed, "Dear Lord, I ain't a rich mouse, or a particularly smart mouse, but I thanks ya for giving me a great family and these new friends to share in our Christmas feast . . . Amen."

Suddenly I seemed to have a lump in my throat . . . I'd never heard such a beautiful prayer.

"Now," said Morton, looking around at everyone slyly, "LET'S EAT!"

The next few minutes were full of happy confusion as the mice family began to pass the bread and cheese around the table, laughing and teasing each other. "Go on . . . have some bread," urged David Mouse, pushing a large crumb onto Matt's bottle cap plate.

Emma, the baby mouse, giggled happily from Mrs. Morton's lap as her daddy tickled her under the chin.

Rebecca leaned close to Matt and whispered, "I can't believe they're so happy! Why, they hardly have enough to eat."

"Yeah," Matt whispered back, "and they don't even have any presents."

"You're right," I whispered to them both, "and didn't I hear somebody say, 'What good is Christmas without a lot of presents?'"

Matt and Rebecca looked at each other and then down at their laps.

Just then we heard a familiar voice calling, "Matt! Rebecca! Time to go home!"

"Sorry, Morton," I said, "we gotta go now."

Matt, Rebecca, and I excused ourselves from the table and headed back toward the mouse hole into my room. Behind us, the whole mouse family waved good-bye from their cheerful, holiday table.

"Thanks for everything," said Matt Mouse in a husky voice.

"Any time!" chuckled Morton, waving good-bye. *"Merry Christmas!"*

"Merry Christmas!" said Rebecca and ducked out of the mouse hole.

"Merry Christmas!" said Matt, also disappearing through the hole.

"Merry Christmas!" I said and reluctantly followed them through the hole. But as I came out of the mouse hole, the room once more began to spin and sparkle around us . . .

Matt and Rebecca were looking around, kind of bewildered. My attic bedroom was its regular size again . . . and so were we—minus the whiskers and mouse tails.

The Secret Adventure was over.

"Man, what a mess!" I murmured, pulling Stanley the stuffed cat out from under a pile of books on the floor. I started picking up the books and putting them on the bookshelf.

Matt and Rebecca leaned against my bed with thoughtful looks on their faces.

"Matt," Rebecca said slowly, "do you feel bad for asking for so much stuff for Christmas."

Matt nodded. "Yeah . . . especially after seeing those mice having a great time together—and they didn't have anything!"

"Except each other," Rebecca reminded him.

Matt gave a big sigh. "Rebecca . . . we really blew it," he admitted.

I opened the steamer trunk and couldn't resist tossing Stanley, the stuffed cat, inside. Then I looked at Matt and Rebecca's long faces. "Well, you know, you still have time to fix it," I said. "There's still two days 'til Christmas."

Just then there was a knock at my bedroom door, and Mrs. Long came in, out of breath. With a rush, Matt and Rebecca threw themselves into her arms, nearly knocking her over.

"Uh . . . hi, kids," she said, stooping down and hugging them back with a surprised smile. "Is this greeting because I actually made it to the top of these steep stairs? Whew, Drea . . . you need mountain climbing gear to get up here to the attic."

"Mom," said Rebecca, "we're sorry for asking for so much for Christmas."

"Yeah," Matt nodded. "We don't need all that stuff."

Mrs. Long looked at Matt and Rebecca, then gave me a strange look. "I must be hallucinating . . . are these *my* children?"

Rebecca laid her head against her mom's shoulder. "We just want to be together—that's all we need."

Mrs. Long drew the kids closer to her. "You're so right . . . that's all we need."

I looked away, almost feeling like I was intruding. Then I heard Mrs. Long say, "Of course, it'll be okay to have a *few* presents, won't it?"

The kids laughed. "But not *too* many," said Matt.

Rebecca gave me a hug and said, "Merry Christmas!" As Matt gave me a good-bye hug, he pulled my head down and whispered, "Thanks, Drea . . . and thank Morton for me, too!"

Then with their usual clatter, Matt and Rebecca disappeared down the stairs toward the first floor.

Mrs. Long shook her head at me in amazement. "How did you *do* that?"

Just then I heard a tiny *squeak, squeak* and saw Morton come out of his hole and dart under the bed . . . and I'm almost positive he winked at me, E.D. I grinned. "Oh," I said, "I had a little help from some friends."

"Well, everyone should have friends like that!" said Mrs. Long and gave me a hug before she followed the kids downstairs.

Whew. Between being chased by a snarling, lip-smacking cat and moving thirty boxes, I'm really ready for that "long winter's nap"—gotta rest up for my stint with the Salvation Army tomorrow, ya know!

But . . . I've been thinking, E.D. Suddenly everything is making sense to me. Grandpa's right—you can't just talk about loving people; you need to live it out! For instance . . . up 'til now I've been wavering between trying to ignore Arlene Blake's stupid jokes—and wanting to give her a taste of her own medicine! But, it's Christmas . . . there's gotta be a different way . . .

Wow! You know, E.D., this *could* be a great Christmas after all!

— *Click!* —

Ooof! Where's the light? . . . there. Just remembered, E.D. Better get that lost sock and overdue library book out from under my bed while I still remember where I found them during our Secret Adventure!

— *Click!* —

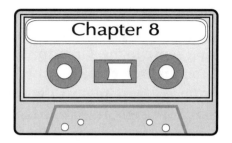

While Visions of Mega-Toys Danced in Their Heads

Day 4,944 in the Secret Adventures of Drea Thomas . . . only two days 'til Christmas and you gotta hear this weather report, E.D. . . . here, just a sec, gotta find the news and weather station . . . oh, here it is . . .

. . . and that's the news on the hour. Bill, do you have a weather report for us?

Sure do, Amanda. Sun, sun, and more sun. Which isn't what the kiddies want to hear who have asked Santa to bring them sleds and ice skates for Christmas this year. But it looks like the Sun Belt is still marching north and covering most of New Jersey and the coastal states . . .

Can you believe it? I thought it just wouldn't

feel like Christmas without snow, but maybe I was wrong . . . well, let me tell you about the day I've had, E.D.

When I got home from working at the Salvation Army store, I was just bursting to tell somebody, but then I remembered that both Kimberly and George were out of town. So, as my trusty *electronic diary*, E.D., you're the lucky—uh—cassette recorder that gets to listen to my latest adventure.

I didn't really know what to expect when I got to the second-hand store. First of all, I knew *zilch* about the Salvation Army, except that they ring bells at Christmas to collect money for the poor. But the lady in charge of the store—Lieutenant Pierce, the one who called me on the phone—was really nice. She wasn't very old, maybe about Mom's age, kinda pretty in her navy, Salvation Army uniform with red trim. She answered all my questions and didn't make me feel dumb or anything—though I kinda felt like I oughta salute or something.

Anyway. Did you know, E.D., that the founders of the Salvation Army . . . oh, what did she say their names were? Oh, yeah, William and Catherine somebody . . . Booth, I think. Anyway, the Booths and their Salvation Army brass band held revival meetings on street corners in England in the 1880s, and the local pub owners hired gangs of thugs to break up the meetings because they were "bad for their liquor business"! But the Salvation Army just kept preaching the Gospel and helping the poor . . . and they're still doing it all over the world more than a hundred years later. Boy, the stuff they don't teach you in school!

End of history lesson, E.D. Lieutenant Pierce gave me a red Santa hat and a red smock to wear over my jeans and baggy shirt . . . I probably looked more like Dopey the Dwarf than one of Santa's elves . . . but anyway. My first job was to put donated stuff on the shelves or in bins and stick prices on them. A lot of it looked like junk to me . . . but Lieutenant Pierce said that if it wasn't broken, *someone* would find a use for it. Stuff that *was* broken I was supposed to put in a storeroom to be repaired.

Like this old desk someone had brought in. Lieutenant Pierce told me to go through it and take out anything left in the drawers, so I tried to open the first drawer—you know, the shallow one in the middle of the desk—and it was really stuck. I pulled and pulled, but it was stuck tight. So then I put one foot on the desk, got both hands on the handle, and gave it a good jerk . . . and that thing suddenly came popping out, sending me flat on my you-know-what with a big crash. At least, I *thought* it was me making the big crash, but when I looked back at the desk, it had totally fallen apart!

Lieutenant Pierce came running to see if I was all right. When she saw the desk all in pieces, she just laughed and said, "Guess that one can go out with the garbage." Then she noticed the drawer I was holding. "Look at that," she said, "all those little cubbyholes dividing the drawer into different sections. That was probably a very nice desk in its day."

So I carried the desk pieces out to the garbage and then set to work on the other donations. Actually, E.D., it was kinda fun sorting through stuff. You wouldn't believe what people "recycle"! There were some really wild hats . . . in fact, I found a great red felt hat to add to my hat collection. There were also a lot of old-fashioned purses—you know, the kind Grandma used to call "pocketbooks" . . . and ceramic figurines—what Grandpa calls "dustables" . . . and shoes and golf clubs and picture frames and toys . . .

Oh. Speaking of toys . . . an elderly woman came in and asked for my help selecting some toys. She had the sweetest smile and kept calling me "Dearie." As we looked at the heap of toys—a Raggedy Ann doll with no hair, a skateboard with all the paint chipped off, puzzles in faded boxes—I felt kinda bad thinking about all the toy commercials her grandkids probably see on TV—you know, "visions of mega-toys" dancing in their heads, courtesy of kid-vid advertising. Then they'll wake up on Christmas morning to second-hand stuff . . .

But the old woman must have been reading my

mind, because she patted my arm and said, "Don't you worry, Dearie . . . there's a gold mine here! I'll take that Raggedy Ann doll . . . why, with a run through the washing machine and some new yarn hair from my sewing bag, she'll be good as new. And that skateboard—look, it has all its wheels. Papa can tighten the screws and give it a coat of blue paint. The kids at Children's Hospital will be delighted."

I was startled. The kids at Children's Hospital?

She smiled at my puzzled expression. "I don't have any children of my own," she explained, rummaging through the toy bin and finding a few more things to buy for a dollar or two, "so I kinda adopt some kids who aren't gonna have much of a Christmas." She beamed at me. "I kinda like fixin' up these toys somebody else has thrown away—it's like coaxing butterflies to come out of their cocoons. Besides," she chuckled, "putting a little somethin' of yourself into a gift . . . isn't that what the spirit of Christmas is all about?"

As she went happily off toward the cash register, I could almost hear Grandpa whispering in my ear, "Love not with words . . . but with actions and truth." I didn't really have time to think about it right then, though, 'cause I got pretty busy—people wanting me to help them find a pair of shoes that fit . . . a lamp that worked . . . even Christmas ornaments for their tree. I did find a big box of ornaments and miniatures that had everything under the sun in it: doll house furniture, tiny musical instruments and tools, miniature toys, a six-inch Christmas tree, little ceramic animals, and even a bride and groom—you know, the sort that stands on top of a wedding cake.

It was the bride and groom that kinda gave me THE IDEA. Ya see, E.D., I had picked them up and set them on the counter, kinda wondering where they came from, when I thought I saw the groom lean over and give the bride a big kiss on the lips . . .

"Oh, honey, not in public!" the bride giggled.

"Well, why not?" protested the groom. "It's our honeymoon . . . we're supposed to kiss in public."

"Hmm, speaking of honeymoons," said the bride, "Ending up in this box of discarded doo-dads isn't exactly what I expected when you promised me a honeymoon I'd never forget."

The groom turned red. "I KNEW we shoulda eloped! But once we got stuck on top of that wedding cake . . . see? I still have stale wedding cake icing stuck to my shoes!"

The brided patted the groom's arm. "Never mind, dear. C'mon . . . whaddya say we get outta here. It's too crowded in this box of junk."

"Good idea!" said the groom. "Let's jet!" And with that, the wedding cake groom swept the bride off her feet, and started to beat a sticky retreat . . . just as a hand reached out and swept them off the counter.

"Oh, where'd you find these, miss?" said a voice. "These would be perfect for my sister's wedding cake! She's getting married on New Year's Eve."

I'd forgotten the young mother with the whining toddler who had been looking through the box for Christmas ornaments.

"Oh . . . that's great," I said. But I felt a little sorry for the old-fashioned bride and groom, once again standing stiffly on their little stand, mutely looking at each other. One more second with my imagination and they'd be off on a well-deserved honeymoon!

But that's when I got my idea, E.D. I've been looking for a special gift in all the wrong places! Suddenly I realized that what I really wanted my gift to say to my special person has been under my nose the whole time . . . and now I know how I want to say it—with a little help from the Salvation Army second-hand store.

As the young mother took her find up to the

cash register, I quickly dug through the box of miniatures 'til I found a few other things—the miniature Christmas tree, a tiny plastic church, a couple of small musical instruments . . . then I made a quick trip out to the garbage.

When I took my loot up to the cash register, Lieutenant Pierce looked amused. "I see you've been doing some shopping yourself, Drea," she said. "Wait a minute . . . what's this? You want to buy this *drawer*? Didn't we put it out in the garbage with the rest of the desk?"

I nodded and grinned. "But like you said, if it's not broken, *someone* can find a use for it."

"That's right, I did," Lieutenant Pierce smiled. "Well, since the drawer no longer has a desk, you can have it for nothing, but . . . the miniatures are twenty-five cents each."

I was so excited about my gift idea, E.D., I could hardly wait for the store to close at four o'clock. Getting the drawer home on my Western Flyer was a juggling act—not to mention getting it into the house without being seen. But Mom wasn't home from work yet . . . Grandpa was whistling in the garage . . . and Dad was pacing in the music room— he always does that when he's writing music. So I managed to get up here to my bedroom without anyone seeing me—I think.

Oh yeah . . . on the way up the back stairs, I moved the Wise Men closer to the kitchen landing.

Tomorrow is Christmas Eve, ya know!

Anyway . . . I've just got tonight and tomorrow to work on my gift. I better get started!

Over and out, E.D.

— *Click!* —

Finally . . . it's Christmas Eve day—otherwise known as Day 4,945 in the Secret Adventures of Drea Thomas . . . and my surprise gift is almost finished! That wedding cake bride and groom at the Salvation Army store started me thinking, E.D., about all the memories they'd have if they could really talk. So I went hunting in our attic, and you'll never believe what I found! Yep . . . Mom and Dad's bride and groom from *their* wedding cake. And that's not all . . . a lot of other little family treasures, long forgotten. But not forgotten for long . . .

One *SNAG*—I've used up all the glue, paste, and rubber cement in the entire house! Wish I could find some more glue somewhere so I wouldn't have to go shopping again . . . Oh, wait. No prob . . . I gotta go shopping anyway! You see, E.D., while I was working on my gift, I got a great idea for how to "get even" with Arlene for all those stupid tricks she's been pulling on me. It's not quite what Kimberly had in mind for "Drea's Revenge" . . . but I guarantee Arlene will be surprised.

— *Click!* —

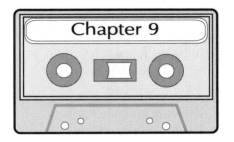

Joy to the World

Merry Christmas, E.D.!

I think I'm the first one up—not counting Morton the mouse, who woke me at six o'clock squeaking under my bed—but I don't mind. I love Christmas morning! Listen . . . I'll open my window. Can you pick up the church bells ringing? . . .

Bong, bong, bong-bong . . . bong-bong, bong, bong . . .

Yeah! They're playing "Joy to the World"! And Christmas carols are playing on the radio . . .

Sigh. There's no better feeling than going downstairs and finding everyone you love around the tree. Makes me want to lean out the window and join the bells singing, "Joy to the World"!

Which reminds me . . . before Grandpa gets

here, I need to move the shepherds and sheep from their "hillside" on the piano to the stable on the mantle . . . After all, it's Christmas morning! They'll want to see the baby Jesus!

— *Click!* —

Back again, E.D.

What a morning! I almost hate for it to end . . . but at least I can tell you about it and relive it a little. I'll back up and start from the beginning.

Grandpa snuck in the back door, all dressed up in a knit vest and red bow tie, and caught me putting all the shepherds around the manger with baby Jesus.

"Merry Christmas, Drea!" he said, coming up behind me and giving me a big bear hug. "Say . . . used to play with that manger scene myself when I was younger 'n you . . . your dad, too." He moved one of the sheep closer to the manger. "Mmm, brings back memories . . . ."

I smiled and kissed his freshly-shaved cheek. Without even knowing it, I'd been taking part in a long family tradition.

"Now," said Grandpa, rubbing his hands gleefully, "while we're waiting for your mom and dad, why don't you and I see if we can put a dent in those cinnamon buns I bought at the bakery on my way over here?"

Pretty soon Dad and Mom came downstairs, still in their robes like me, and helped polish off the cinnamon buns along with the fresh coffee and orange juice that Grandpa and I fixed.

"Now," Dad said, plonking himself down beside the Christmas tree and rubbing his hands together gleefully—I was beginning to see a family resemblance here, E.D.—"can we open the presents yet?"

"Sounds good to me," Mom said, settling into one of our high-backed, Victorian chairs. She looked so young and excited with that big ribbon tying back her hair. "Who's going to go first?" she asked.

I sat down on the matching footstool by Mom's chair and watched Grandpa pick a gift from under the tree and hand it to Mom. "Ask and you shall receive," he said, his eyes twinkling. "Here's one with your name on it, Laurie."

"Oh, goody," Mom said, grinning. She quickly undid the wrapping, opened the box inside, and lifted out a gleaming, handmade, wooden box.

"A jewelry box!" Mom breathed, gently opening the top and looking in. I peeked around the wrapping and saw beautiful blue velvet cloth lining the inside. "It even has a place for my earrings!" Mom exclaimed. "Oh, Ben . . . you put a lot of time into making this."

So that was what Grandpa was doing in the garage all this past week!

Grandpa kinda shrugged shyly. "Now you know why I kept turning down your dinner invitations."

"Well, I love it," said Mom, running her fingers gently over the polished wood, then holding it up for all of us to see. It was absolutely beautiful, made of smooth, varnished wood stained a rich, maple color, with tiny gold hinges on the back and inlaid, polished wood arranged in a decorative pattern on top. Mom's eyes were shining.

"I love it, too!" I said. "Now I can always find Mom's earrings when I want to borrow them!"

Mom gave me a look that said don't-push-your-luck-kiddo. "Maybe you could put a little lock on this for me," she said pointedly, looking at Grandpa.

"You got it!" Grandpa chuckled. "Coming up for your birthday."

"Well," said Dad, wiggling his bushy eyebrows as a broad hint, "who's next?"

"How 'bout Drea?" Mom said, pointing eagerly to a small, square gift with a lot of lacy ribbon.

Honestly, E.D., Dad was acting like a little kid. He stuck out his lip in a mock pout that it wasn't his turn yet. But I ignored him and carefully undid the ribbon and paper, opened the box inside . . . and lifted out a vaguely familiar old-fashioned watch, with a lovely, new, ribbon-and-lace band.

I looked at Mom wide-eyed. "Oh, Mom . . . it's your first watch!"

She smiled and nodded, pleased that I remembered it. "It needed a cleaning and a new band, but it still keeps pretty good time."

In the back of my mind, I wondered if it told twenty-four-hour time like my neon-colored morphing watch . . . then decided that with a little imagination, the new watch could tell time however I wanted it to.

"Are you sure you want to give it to me?" I asked, knowing how much that watch meant to my Mom.

Mom nodded. "My mother gave it to me when I was your age . . . now I want you to have it."

Talk about a gift from the heart, E.D. . . . I felt like Mom was sharing part of herself, passing a family treasure down from one generation to the next. "I love it!" I said, trying it on.

"Oh, that's not all . . . there's something else in there," Mom hinted.

I reached back into the box and pulled out a heart-shaped card. " 'Let Our Hours be Ours,' " I read out loud, and opened the card. Inside it said, " 'This coupon entitles the bearer, Drea Thomas, to thirteen uninterrupted Mom/Daughter hours—one hour for each Christmas we've spent together.' "

I looked at Mom. Her eyes were shining. "I love you, Mom," I said, giving her a hug. I am *definitely* going to cash these coupons in!

Then I jumped up. "This is so much fun! Wait, everybody . . . I'll be right back."

I ran out of the room to get my gift, which I'd left out in the hall, because I didn't want anyone to see the giftwrap, either.

"Must be something big," I heard Mom say.

"Oh, goody, it's for me!" Dad said, rubbing his hands together again as I came back in.

"How do you know?" Mom teased. "Grandpa hasn't opened a gift yet, either."

"It's gotta be for me," Dad protested. "You and Drea have already opened one and I didn't draw my own name—that was against the rules, remember?"

Well, E.D., Dad was right—my gift *was* for him. I put the large package in his arms and waited to see his reaction.

Dad's eyes were as wide as silver dollars. "Wow!" he said, looking at the brown, paper bag wrapping I'd used, complete with red and green sponge-painted decorations. "This is great! I don't know what's inside, but I sure like the outside."

My heart was really beating hard, E.D. *Would* he like it? It *was* a little bit odd, I had to admit, but it *was* from the heart.

By this time Dad had the wrapping off, exposing the bottom of the old drawer from the Salvation Army desk. "Wow," he murmured, "a drawer . . ."

I rolled my eyes. "Turn it over, Dad."

Dad gently turned the drawer over . . . and there, for everyone to see, was the shadowbox I'd created from the old drawer with all the little compartments. The tiny Christmas tree was in the top left corner, with cotton "snow" piled around its base . . . next to it was a family portrait of Dad, Mom, me, and Grandpa in a "new" frame I'd made out of some rough wood pieces from Grandpa's workbench . . . in the middle left compartment was a page from Grandma's Bible, which was falling apart, but which Dad couldn't bear to throw away, along with the tiny plastic church and a Bible and a cross I had cut out from our church bulletins . . . next to that was the first piano piece Dad ever wrote for me, along with the little plastic instruments I'd found at the Salvation army store . . .

Grandpa leaned in for a closer look, and grinned when he saw the little silver trophy in the bottom left corner. "Yep," I said, "that's the trophy you gave Dad when I was born."

Grandpa chuckled. "Yep . . . I told him you would always be his greatest 'achievement.' "

"And that's the bride and groom from our wedding cake!" Mom exclaimed. "Where did you find that? I thought it was lost years ago!"

The final compartment was filled with dried flowers and leaves from our back yard, with one of my miniature bunnies and a tiny straw hat peeking out from the bottom.

Dad was speechless. I could tell he liked it. Finally he stammered, "I—I don't know what to say."

"Say 'thank you,' " Mom prompted gently.

Dad's voice got a little husky. "Honey," he said to me, "I think this is the most special gift I have ever received . . ." and he gave me a big, daddy hug.

"Well!" said Dad, "I don't know how I'm supposed to follow that, but . . ." He reached under the Christmas tree and handed a flat package to Grandpa. "Merry Christmas, Dad."

"Thank you, Son," said Grandpa, testing the weight and size of the package. "Can't be golf balls," he chuckled.

Dad shook his head. "You'll never guess. But . . . I really wish I could have done this while Mom was still alive." Dad's voice cracked a little, which often happens when he talks about Grandma Thomas, even though she died about ten years ago.

Mom and I almost held our breath as Grandpa took off the wrapping paper, revealing a beautiful leather binder. Some words were embossed in gold lettering on the cover.

" 'The Benjamin Thomas Suite . . . Ode to a Railroad Man,' " Grandpa read. He looked at Dad. "You wrote me a symphony?" he asked, astonished.

Dad was grinning from ear to ear. "That's not all," he cried, jumping to his feet. "I even got the Hampton Falls College orchestra to record it for their final exam!"

With that, he stepped through the arch into the music room, where he'd set up a tape player and speakers on the piano, and punched the "play" button. A whole orchestra of strings, woodwinds, brass, and percussion instruments began playing the stirring sounds of Dad's "Ode to a Railroad Man."

Grandpa leaned back in the other high-back Victorian chair, a look of wonder on his face as he listened to the music, which reminded me a little of Copeland's *Appalachian Spring* . . . but different. Behind the cheerful strings, we could hear a plaintive, *whooshing* sound—like the passing of a train. Mom and I looked at each other with big grins . . . what a wonderful present Dad had created!

As the rich, full music swelled in the room, Grandpa looked at all of us, his eyes bright, and said, "I don't know about you folks, but . . . this is the best Christmas I can ever remember."

I think he's right, E.D.

Anyway. After listening to the whole symphony

piece, we got dressed to go to the Christmas service at church. Guess I better see if everyone else is ready—

Riiiiiinnnnnnnggggg.

Huh? Who in the world would be calling us Christmas morning?

— *Click!* —

Shoulda known, E.D. That was Kimberly, calling to wish me Merry Christmas . . . *and* to tell me that it's *snowing* in the Poconos. Can you believe it?! She didn't have to rub it in.

Anyway. She asked if anything else had happened about Arlene's threat to ruin my Christmas . . . so I told her about the thirty boxes of Surfin' Santas and volunteering me at the Salvation Army. To my surprise, Kimberly started laughing. "I've got to hand it to Arlene," she said between giggles. "I didn't think she'd get so creative!"

Well. I didn't think it was so funny, but . . . pretty soon I started laughing, too. So then I told Kimberly that I had a good idea for how to get even with Arlene—but I didn't tell her what. She'd probably try to talk me out of it.

But if my idea works, E.D., it'll really make this a "right" Christmas!—

Oh, I hear Dad calling. Time to leave for church. Over and out.

— *Click!* —

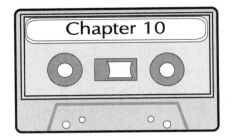

Chapter 10

I Wish You a Merry Christmas

Late Christmas afternoon . . . Day 4,946 in the Secret Adventures of Drea Thomas . . . and boy, E.D., did this ever turn out to be a "right" Christmas!

For one thing, somewhere between the time we came home from church and the time we finished Christmas dinner, the temperature dropped at least forty degrees. *At last* the weather decided to act like December twenty-fifth . . . guess it's better late than never!

For another thing, Matt and Rebecca came over with a gift for me . . . wow! I couldn't believe it! It was a cool red hat and plaid scarf to match the red winter coat which has been hanging forlornly in the closet since Mom got it for me a month ago. Perfect timing! They were so excited . . . they're really into gift *giving* now.

Last but not least, I had one more Christmas thing to do this afternoon. It was a bit too cold for biking, so I decided a nice crisp walk would feel good after Mom's turkey dinner with all the trimmings, and Dad's special blackberry pie. I looked up Arlene Blake's address in the phone book . . . and almost asked Grandpa to drive me. She lives clear on the other side of town! But . . . no, this was something I had to do by myself.

It was funny walking through downtown Hampton Falls on Christmas Day. All the stores were closed . . . the streets practically deserted. All the hype and ho-ho-ho's were finally silent. Even the Salvation Army bell ringers were gone. It was kinda peaceful in a way . . .

The thirty-degree temperature kept me walking fast to keep warm, and pretty soon I found myself in a neighborhood full of new, split-level houses. It was kinda eerie . . . the place seemed completely deserted. Finally I saw a few kids through the windows, still in their pajamas, playing with their Christmas toys. But everything was so quiet.

Too quiet. I got to thinking, what if Arlene wasn't home, and I had walked all the way over here for nothing?

I checked the address I had written down, and

sure enough, there was her house with a curved sidewalk going up to the front door.

On the way up the walk, my foot hit a patch of ice but I caught myself before I went down. *Hey, that's great!* I thought. *Maybe it'll stay cold enough for the city to flood the ice rink in the park, and we can go ice skating before school opens!*

But I didn't have much time to think about ice skating. Actually, I was pretty nervous, and for a brief second I was tempted to turn around and walk home. But my finger was on auto-pilot and rang the doorbell before I had a chance to reconsider.

Guess who opened the door? Arlene herself . . . wearing an expensive red ski sweater, light blue stretch pants, and a white bow tying up her blond hair. Probably some of the Christmas "presents" that she bought herself.

"Hi," I said. It was all I could think of to say.

Her eyes narrowed. "What do you want?" she asked suspiciously.

I held out the shiny, green gift bag I was carrying in my mittened hand.

"I don't want a gift from you!" Arlene snapped, and would have slammed the door in my face . . . except just then this gorgeous woman with blonde hair swept up in a french twist appeared in the doorway.

"Oh, Arlene," said Mrs. Blake, "did one of your

friends bring you a gift?" she said, and smiled at me sweetly.

"She's *not* my friend," Arlene said icily.

Mrs. Blake shook her head, still smiling, as though partly embarrassed and partly amused by Arlene's rudeness. "You'd never know she was at the top of her charm school class, would you?" she half-apologized.

Arlene rolled her eyes. "Mother, *please*," she said.

Mrs. Blake placed both hands on Arlene's shoulders and gave her a little push. "Arlene," she said firmly, her voice still dripping honey, "please be the daughter that I raised you to be and graciously accept your friend's gift."

I was beginning to enjoy this conversation. So far I'd only had to say one word. At Mrs. Blake's cue, I held out the gift bag once more. Gritting her teeth, Arlene snatched it out of my hand and gingerly reached inside . . . probably expecting to plunge her hand into wet noodles or peeled grapes.

Instead she pulled out a small velvet box and stared at it in astonishment. " 'Hampton Falls Jewelry'?" she read off the top of the box.

I just smiled.

Arlene opened the velvet box and her eyes popped a little more. Her mother peered curiously over her shoulder.

"Oh . . . a beautiful, crystal 'A' initial pin," Mrs. Blake breathed. "What do you say, dear?"

Arlene looked really confused. But she still gagged on the words. "Th—thank you," she finally said reluctantly.

Satisfied, Mrs. Blake disappeared back into the house.

"You're welcome," I said . . . then added, "Merry Christmas!"

It was over . . . and Grandpa was right. The best way to defuse a nasty situation was to show love with actions . . . even to someone like Arlene. I turned and walked back down the sidewalk.

Arlene must have recovered from the shock, because the next moment I heard her yell behind me, "Wait a minute! This is a trick, isn't it?" I heard footsteps starting to run down the walk after me. "Well, I'm not going to fall for it—aaaiiiieeee!"

At Arlene's scream, I whirled around just in time to see her legs fly out from under her. She landed right on her tail bone with a sickening *THUD!* next to the little patch of ice on the sidewalk.

I rushed over to her side. "Arlene!" I cried. "Are you all right?"

"*Yes!*" screamed Arlene. "I'm fine! Just leave me alone—oooohhhh." She writhed on the ground.

It was obvious that she wasn't all right. Quickly I ran back into the house calling for Mrs. Blake. Behind me, Arlene was so mad I thought she was going to explode like a box of lit fireworks. In fact, I can still hear her last words to me ringing out clearly in the cold, December air:

"Drea Thomas . . . I hate you!"

Sigh. I tried, E.D., I really did. I still think returning good for bad was the best way to turn Arlene's stupid pranks into a "right" Christmas. I mean, how was I to know that Arlene would slip on the only patch of ice in all of Hampton Falls! Hmmm . . . I wonder if that means her ski vacation to Aspen just got "latered"?

Speaking of Aspen . . . why is it so cold up here in my attic room? The furnace has been working overtime all afternoon, trying to catch up with the sudden drop in temperature . . . but it's still kinda cold in here. I think some cocoa and Christmas cookies sound like a good way to warm up.

Over and out, E.D.

— *Click!* —

Forget cold. I got a hot idea!—the perfect thing to top off a perfect Christmas!

Ya see, I had just poured myself a mug of milk and popped it into the microwave, and was just standing there thinkin' . . . wondering how the kids at Children's Memorial liked the gifts the old lady fixed up for them from the Salvation Army store. I realized the job she was trying to do was a pretty big one . . . just her and "Papa"—that must be her husband—trying to help dozens of kids at the hospital have a happy Christmas. I was just wishing I'd found out her name, thinking that it might be fun to help her fix up toys next year, when the toaster on the counter morphed right in front of me . . .

"So, Drea!" said the gravelly voice of my friend, Mr. Toaster. He was wearing a fuzzy, red Santa hat slouched over one side of his slots. "Whaddya gonna do with all the money you saved by drawing names this Christmas?"

"Money?" I echoed. "Hmmm . . . you're right. I did save quite a bit of baby-sitting money for Christmas and ended up using only part of it."

"Well— cough, cough— Christmas isn't over yet," hinted the toaster. "You could still get your ol' friend something nice . . . wrap it up in Christmas paper . . . tie it with a bow . . ."

I shrugged. "Sorry, Toaster. It's Christmas Day . . . the stores aren't open."

"Oh. Well!" he huffed. "Couldn't you come up with somethin'? You've got a whole garage full of

brand-new toys . . ."

I looked at the toaster in amazement. "Toaster, you're brilliant!" I cried. "That's it! That's the perfect solution!"

Forgetting my hot milk in the microwave, I made a mad dash for the back stairs up to my room.

"What did I do? Solution to what?" the toaster called out after me. "Well, yes, brilliant for sure, but . . ."

Now all I've got to do, E.D., is find my purse and see how much money I've got left . . . and then find Mom and Dad and Grandpa, and see if they'll go along with my idea . . . now, where did I leave that purse . . .?

Found it. Okay, here goes . . . let's see . . . twenty . . . twenty-five . . . thirty-five . . . forty . . . fifty . . . fifty-one . . . fifty-two . . . *yes!* That's it! I'm sure it'll be enough!

— *Click!* —

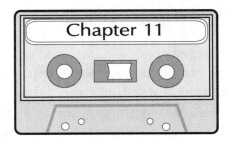

Chapter 11

Winter Wonderland

Back again, E.D. Whew! What a day! Just when I thought it was over, it suddenly took off in another whirlwind. But it's now twenty-one-hundred hours—that's nine o'clock to humdrum humans—and I'm back in my room, sitting on my window seat, and I'll try to catch you up on what happened . . .

Okay. I found Mom and Dad and Grandpa in the living room, enjoying another fire in the fireplace—courtesy of the old cherry tree—and I presented my idea kinda all in one breath.

Dad scratched his head. "Now, how is this idea of yours gonna get paid for again?" he asked, wrinkling his forehead.

"Well, ya see," I said, taking a big breath, "since those Surfin' Santas cost a hundred and ninety-two dollars . . . "

"*And* thirty-six cents," Grandpa reminded me.

"Oh. Right," I said, grabbing a piece of paper and doing some quick figuring. "Okay . . . a hundred and ninety-two dollars *and* thirty-six cents divided four ways would be forty-eight dollars and nine cents apiece. Since we all saved money by drawing just one name for Christmas this year . . ." —I went for the hard sell— ". . . we could all afford to buy those Surfin' Santas and—"

"*Buy* them?" Dad interrupted. "Why in the world would we do that?"

What he really meant, E.D., was why in the world would we do something that stupid.

"As I was saying," I said, ignoring Dad's comment, "we could all afford to buy those Surfin' Santas and take them down to Children's Memorial, because the old lady in the Salvation Army store probably couldn't fix up enough toys for all the kids who have to be in the hospital over Christmas Day and—

"Whoa, whoa, whoa," said Mom, laughing. "What in the world are you talking about?"

So I had to back up and tell them all about my day at the Salvation Army store and the nice, old lady who bought second hand toys and fixed them up but didn't have any children of her own so she "adopted" kids at the hospital . . .

"And we've got a whole garage full of brand-new toys that could make a lot of kids happy," I finished, pulling a wad of money out of my pants pocket. "Here's my share, Grandpa . . . I guess we should each pay you, since you already paid for the whole shipment."

Mom and Dad and Grandpa looked at each other . . . and I'm sure I saw those little Christmas light bulbs go off over their heads again as my idea sank in.

"It's a good idea," Dad said slowly. "Toys, yes, but . . . Surfin' Santas?"

"Well, I'm all for it," Mom said, getting up and going for her purse. "Here you are, Ben . . . forty-eight dollars."

"*And* nine cents," Grandpa said, his eyes twinkling, as he held out his hand.

Well, anyway, E.D. . . . to make a long story short, we dragged all those Surfin' Santa dolls out of the garage and used up all the Christmas paper gift wrapping them. As we were wrapping the last few, Grandpa held one up and said, "Are you sure that we shouldn't return these guys?"

"Noooooo," I said patiently, sticking tape on both ends of the package in my hands. "Like I said, with the money that our family saved on gifts, we can all pitch in a few bucks and take good ol' Surfin' St. Nick to the Children's Hospital. Tonight."

Grandpa eyed the doll critically. "Hmmm . . . I dunno."

"Whoa, whoa, whoa! What happened to 'love not with words, but with actions'?" I pointed out.

Grandpa laughed. "You're right. Ya don't forget a thing, do you, Drea? . . . Are we done here? Okay, let's load 'em in my car."

He eyed the last Surfin' Santa before it disappeared into the gift wrap . . . then let loose with a very un-Grandpa-like, "*Cowabunga!*"

I teased him about it all the way to the hospital . . . told him he'd been watching too many Ninja Turtle reruns.

They weren't expecting us at the hospital . . . but the security guard steered us to a head nurse, who was very helpful. I thought maybe we'd just leave the toys and the nurses could hand them out, but the head nurse encouraged us to hand out the packages personally. She even loaned us a gurney—ya know, those high, flat beds on wheels you see on TV shows like "ER: Emergency Room"—to wheel the gifts down the halls.

As we went room to room, Grandpa really got into the spirit of things. He'd peek into a room, then wheel in the gurney with a "Ho-ho-ho!" Most of the kids looked pretty skeptical about this "Santa Claus" with a red bow tie, suspenders, and no beard . . . but they smiled real big when we handed out the Surfin' Santa dolls, and begged us to stay awhile.

So it took longer than I thought, and I'm pretty tired now. But I feel good . . . and even though it hasn't been a "white" Christmas, it's definitely been a "right" Christmas—

Knock, knock.

Oh, hi, Grandpa . . . come on in. I was just describing our trip to the children's hospital for my electronic diary . . .

— *Click!* —

Back again, E.D. Grandpa came up to my room to say goodnight before going home to his apartment. We sat on my window seat together, just looking out the window and sharing the last moments of the day.

"Don't you want to open the window?" Grandpa suggested.

"Open the window?" I asked. "Well, sure . . . ."

We opened the double dormer windows and just leaned on the window sill, looking out. I noticed that it had gotten cloudy . . . too bad, I thought, 'cause now we couldn't see the Christmas star.

Then behind us we heard Dad and Mom coming into my room quietly, saying, "Merry Christmas!"

Grandpa and I grinned and tried to make room for them on the window seat. The more the merrier!

Then Dad nudged me. "Look outside."

I looked and my eyes widened. It was snowing!

"Merry Christmas!" we said, laughing and hugging each other as the fluffy white flakes floated gently down from the pearl gray sky. "Merry Christmas! . . . Merry Christmas! . . . Merry Christmas!"

Sigh. Now Grandpa's gone home, and Mom and Dad are in bed. It's twenty-two-thirty hours, E.D., no creatures are stirring—not even Morton the mouse. Guess it's time for me to duck under the covers, too. But . . . just wanted to say that the last *SNAG* in Day 4,946 in the Secret Adventures of Drea Thomas has finally unraveled . . .

It's a real winter wonderland out there.
— *Click!* —

Telling Time the
Secret Adventures Way!

Use the following chart to tell time like Drea's Mighty Morphing Watch!

(*Note:* "Military time" is based on a 24-hour day—unlike "civilian time," which is based on two 12-hour time periods).

12-hour clock	*24-hour clock*
1 o'clock a.m.	0100 hours (oh-one-hundred hours)
2 o'clock a.m.	0200 hours (oh-two-hundred hours)
3 o'clock a.m.	0300 hours (oh-three-hundred hours)
4 o'clock a.m.	0400 hours (oh-four-hundred hours)
5 o'clock a.m.	0500 hours (oh-five-hundred hours)

6 o'clock a.m.	0600 hours (oh-six-hundred hours)
7 o'clock a.m.	0700 hours (oh-seven-hundred hours)
8 o'clock a.m.	0800 hours (oh-eight-hundred hours)
9 o'clock a.m.	0900 hours (oh-nine-hundred hours)
10 o'clock a.m.	1000 hours (ten-hundred hours)
11 o'clock a.m.	1100 hours (eleven-hundred hours)
12 o'clock p.m.	1200 hours (twelve-hundred hours)

Watch out! Here's where it gets tricky!

1 o'clock p.m.	1300 hours (thirteen-hundred hours)
2 o'clock p.m.	1400 hours (fourteen-hundred hours)
3 o'clock p.m.	1500 hours (fifteen-hundred hours)
4 o'clock p.m.	1600 hours (sixteen-hundred hours)
5 o'clock p.m.	1700 hours (seventeen-hundred hours)
6 o'clock p.m.	1800 hours (eighteen-hundred hours)
7 o'clock p.m.	1900 hours (nineteen-hundred hours)
8 o'clock p.m.	2000 hours (twenty-hundred hours)
9 o'clock p.m.	2100 hours (twenty-one-hundred hours)
10 o'clock p.m.	2200 hours (twenty-two-hundred hours)
11 o'clock p.m.	2300 hours (twenty-three-hundred hours)
12 o'clock a.m.	2400 hours (twenty-four-hundred hours)

Minutes in between hours are described like this:

10:15 a.m.	1015 hours (ten-fifteen-hundred hours)
6:30 p.m.	1830 hours (eighteen-thirty-hundred hours)

In everyday speech, the words "hours" or "hundred hours" are often dropped. (E.g., "Meet me at school at oh-eight-hundred, okay?" "Be home for chow at eighteen-thirty—sharp!")

DAY
4,134

Figure Your Age the
Secret Adventures Way

Want to know how many days old you are?
Here's how . . .
1. Multiply your age by 365 days. (For example:
   There are 365 days in each year. If you are 11
   years old, multiply 365 x 11 = 4,015.)
2. Next, add one day for every "leap year"
   you've been alive. (Note: every fourth year has
   an extra day in February, or 366 days, which is

called leap year.) Here are some current leap years: 1980, 1984, 1988, 1992, 1996, 2000.

3. Now get a calendar (you may need last year's calendar, too, if you haven't had your birthday yet this year) and count how many days it's been since your LAST birthday until TODAY.

4. Add your totals from Steps 1, 2, and 3. (For example: 4,015, plus 3 leap years ['84, '88, and '92], plus, say, 116 days since your last birthday = today would be Day 4,134 in the Secret Adventures of You!)